Sherry & Narcotics

a novel by Nina-Marie Gardner

Future Fiction London

SHERRY AND NARCOTICS
By Nina-Marie Gardner
Published 2011 by Future Fiction London
www.futurefiction.co.uk
ISBN 978-0-9827928-2-7

Cover art by STEVE BYRAM
Cover design by Gilded Peony
Author photo by NI RONG

Sherry & Narcotics

a novel by Nina-Marie Gardner

Future Fiction London

For Rach & Gwyn
(& eternal thanks to my family)

Oh what a dear ravishing thing is the beginning of an Amour!

—Aphra Behn, *The Emperor of the Moon*

1.

October. Mary is on the noon express out of London hurtling towards Manchester Piccadilly. She sits by the window, knees up against the seat in front of her. Stares out at the countryside - so many patch-worked fields and hedges, factory smokestacks and church spires silhouetted against the sky. So many rows upon rows of identical houses, all of them made of stone. It's one of the first things she notices in this country - so few buildings made of wood.

Just over three weeks she's been corresponding with Jake. He reaches out to her first. He likes her plays, she likes his poems, they have mutual friends. Now they are going to meet. From his photos he's gorgeous, but she's allowed plenty of room in her expectations. She won't be easily shaken if he's not. He could be fat with a weak chin and bad teeth and she'd still be smitten. He wins her easily with his words. It happens lightening fast. She's alone abroad and she wants it.

Thinking about him on the train makes her giddy, sends a shudder down her spine. Has her craving her next drink, a cigarette.

Checks the time on her cell phone and sighs. It's ten past one. Lately she's been trying hard not to drink before it gets dark out. She has to be careful.

'If you started drinking again, I think it would kill your mother,' her Uncle George says when she meets him for lunch a week earlier. They are at the restaurant of his hotel in Mayfair. He's in London on some mission with his church group from South Carolina. Inside Mary's cringing because he thinks she's been sober for years.

'Anyway, everyone is so proud of you,' he continues. 'You look well.' He's all concerned but his eyes are twinkling. He reminds her of Bill Clinton.

'Yea, thanks,' she replies. 'You too.' Sitting there in the wide booth she feels especially small.

The maitre d' hands her a glossy menu the size of a school lunch tray. Holding it in front of herself, she might be in her own private room, one with walls that read 'Escallopes de Mer' and 'Braised Liver Rangoons.'

'Phew!' says George.

'Indeed.' She feels his eyes on her, taking her in - nothing gets by him. He happens to be an expert on deviants, juvenile delinquents, youths that have problems with drugs and alcohol. In his hometown he's a crusader, has a hand in all kinds of campaigns. His favorite is 'Say No to Drugs.'

Mary's not stupid. She knows why her mother has sent him. He's checking up. She's dressed in her best Ann Taylor 'Ivy League graduate and now I'm a vague type of consultant' ensemble, just to fool him. Cream-colored blouse with a Peter Pan collar. Black velvet headband. Fitted tweed skirt. Mary Jane pumps.

Even dug up the pearls her father brought back from one of his trips to China. The ones he gave her when she graduated high school. Only now, more than a decade later, she's wearing them for the very first time.

'Why don't we go ahead and order,' George says. Leans in close, she smells the mint on his breath. 'Then we'll catch up.' And he winks.

Mary resists the urge to turn around like the wink was meant for someone behind her. Be kind, she tells herself. Just get through this.

A successful lunch with her uncle means a stretch of time she won't have to communicate with her mother. A few weeks spared of having to answer for, explain, or deny what she may or may not be doing in London.

Since her father died, Mary finds she alternately craves and is repulsed by her mom. She doesn't understand it, and it fills her with shame. Underneath she loves her, feels for her powerfully. Misses her. But lately, any form of contact is too much. Her mother's voice on the phone enrages her, makes her wish she'd never picked up, never succumbed to the impulse to call.

'Mary? Why don't you start.'

The waiter is standing before them, and Uncle George nods kindly at her.

Bless him, Mary thinks. She's starving and eating will stop her hands from shaking. She's dead sober and well-rested but self-consciousness is getting the better of her. She might have a panic attack. She scopes out the signs for the ladies room, the exits.

'I'll have the Caesar salad.'

'Croque Monsieur,' says Uncle George, grinning, patting his sizeable belly. He is a large man. 'Your Aunt Lorraine wouldn't approve, my cholesterol, you know. But when in London…'

'Or France,' Mary says with a smile.

'So, your mother tells me you finished your degree?'

'Yes.'

'That's just wonderful. Congratulations. So what are your plans?'

'Yea, um, you know...' Mary reaches for the breadbasket. She's surviving on a budget of five pounds a day so the free lunch means she'll finish out ahead. Still, she's running out of money.

'You're working, I take it?'

'Consulting.'

Mary loves that word, as much as she hates it. Loves using it on Uncle George - she's speaking his language. Everybody is a consultant these days. As far as Mary is concerned it has to be the most bullshit title on the planet.

Her income consists of the money she makes rewriting papers for an online essay mill. 'Get an Ivy League mind behind your application essay,' is the company motto. She likes the idea of pimping her brain. Most of all she loves the freedom it gives her. She could edit her essays from Mars as long as there's an internet connection. It's how she's been able to stay in the UK since her student visa ran out. Now, as long as she pays a visit to Paris or Berlin every couple of weeks, she can live in London as an outlaw.

'Tell me about what it is you do,' Uncle George is saying with his most meaningful look.

'Ah...I work with kids from all over the world - but mainly China. Help them with their essays for college or grad school.'

'You don't write their essays for them?'

Again, Mary must resist the urge to do or say something rude. Instead she smiles. 'Gosh, no.'

She thinks, of course I write their essays for them. But it's more complicated than that. Every day she climbs inside the lives of six to eight students from Beijing to Kazakhstan. Untangles their words and rearranges them in the style preferred by places like Harvard and Yale.

George raises an eyebrow. 'Well that's great, Mary. And how's the playwriting going?'

This stings. The one-act she completed for her degree has been rejected by every theater company, large and small, in London. And her full-length effort is stalled - she can't see beyond the opening scene, where the prodigal, drug-addled daughter returns home after the death of her father, much to the horror of her long-suffering mother.

'Oh you know,' she says. 'I'm working on this new piece that's sort of been informally commissioned by this company in Manchester.'

It's a flat-out lie, but Uncle George has already lost interest.

'I'm hoping they might want to do it in Edinburgh. We'll see,' she continues.

'What about theater in the States? I thought you'd want to move right back to New York.'

'Ugh, no,' Mary starts, but she can't explain it. Doesn't want to, not to Uncle George. The room is too warm and her head hurts. 'Excuse me, I'm just going to run to the ladies room. I'll be right back.'

Once she is locked in a stall with a faucet left on at full blast, she drops her head between her knees and starts taking deep breaths.

Mary lifts her head from the train window and peers out over the tops of the seats in front of her. A man in uniform is struggling with a large cart, trying to maneuver it between the sliding doors that separate the train carriages. She can see the wine bottles amidst the packets of crisps and biscuits, knows there are cold cans of lager in its refrigerated compartments.

Checks her mobile phone; now it's nearly two o'clock. She's thirsty. When the cart reaches her, she pulls her wallet from her knapsack.

'A Carlsburg?' she says, like he's going to tell her no. She speaks quickly, as has become her habit - it helps mask her accent.

'Excuse me?'

'Um,' Mary's caught. She must spell it out - or order a Coke or a coffee instead. 'Car-uls-berg?' she says again, looking up at him hopefully.

'Ah!' the man smiles. He's found her out. 'All right-y. That'll be three pounds.' He says it cheerfully - she might be having a lollipop. He hands her the cold beer, and once he and the cart have disappeared into the next car, she opens it and takes a sip.

The alcohol curls out from her heart to her extremities. With just that first sip she can feel it in her wrists, her fingers. An excited sort of itch. Takes another and stares out the window.

The last time she saw her Uncle George. Before London. Before she went to rehab. At the funeral in Washington DC. Her father's work for the Attorney General earns him a place in Arlington Cemetery - and a full military sendoff, with the horses and cannons and troops in uniform - the works.

Mary is the only person he recognizes at the end. They giggle at his nurse, who worships Oprah and even talks to her on the TV like they are old friends. When he first gets sick, Mary smuggles him cigarettes. They smoke out back, in the hospital parking lot, her dad in a wheelchair. The natural light brings out all the yellow in his skin. He is diagnosed with late stage pancreatic cancer in July and by the following February he is dead. With the weight loss, the faded smocks, his hair missing in places and growing back in odd tufts, the way he becomes all veins, he reminds her of a large baby bird. But still, he smiles at her like her old dad. They have the same dark eyes, the same mischievous grin.

Those days, when her father is dying, Mary tears it up in Manhattan. Everything happens at once: her dad gets sick, she splits with the only boy she thinks she'll ever love, her first play is produced and flops. Her father never gets to see it, and she doesn't tell him about the reviews.

He keeps saying it's never too late to go to business school. That he could see her working someplace like Google.

She tries cocaine and ecstasy for the first time and never stops. Loses her nerve and isn't sure she ever wants to write again. Can only shrug at what she once dreamed of. Takes a job her dad is proud of, working for one of his Yale classmates, executive recruiting on Wall Street. Spends her nights running wild, snorting drugs, popping pills and hooking up with strangers, trying to reach some sort of sublime oblivion.

Sundays - and more frequently as her dad grows sicker - she takes the shuttle to Washington to sit with him in the hospital. She and her mother are like satellites, both orbiting around her father, but spinning in opposition to each other. Her mother doesn't say anything but she knows Mary has a drug problem. They both know it's going to be an issue once her father is gone.

In the seven months it takes for the cancer to kill him, Mary distances herself from most of the people in her life who truly care about her. Around the time he dies, all she has left are her drug dealers and strangers.

She wants only to be at his side when he goes. That night she's in New York. Planning to stay in, except she lets herself be talked into going out. Winds up chatting to a beautiful black woman in the ladies room of some trendy lounge on the Lower East Side. Next thing she knows she's doing cocaine with the girl off the toilet paper dispenser. Then giggling by the mirror as they wash their hands and clear their nostrils. Then locked back in the stall doing more cocaine. Then kissing. Then fingering each other.

They make out and fool around for a while. All Mary wants is the girl and more cocaine. But instead the girl gets this crazy wired grin and drags Mary out to meet her boyfriend, who turns out to be this big German guy. Mary dislikes him instantly but it doesn't matter, his girlfriend is so hot. Mary isn't gay and she never considered herself particularly bi, but coked up and in pain as she is, she wants something soft and resplendent with beauty. This girl takes her hand and her eyes are like exotic birds, her skin the smoothest salve, her tongue the most tender comfort Mary has ever known.

Back at their flat, a windowless one bedroom somewhere on Orchard Street, nobody even bothers to turn on the lights. They just go at it. Mary feels like a sacrifice.

Only when she opens her eyes the next morning, the three of them intertwined naked on the bed, does she spring up in a panic. *Oh my God! Dad!* Crawling nude on her hands and knees on the floor until she locates her clothes, her purse, her phone.

It's nine in the morning.

Her voicemail-box is full and she's missed too many calls from her mother to count.

She might have even started to cry right then, she is hysterical. Wrapping her coat around herself, she runs down two flights of stairs and bursts out into the empty street. Hails a cab. There's no time to go home, to shower, to change, or pack a bag. Listens to her mother's messages as the cab races to La Guardia. Her father is dead.

Only when she's walking down the endless arrivals corridor at Washington National, her hands jammed in her pockets, does she find the small vial. Her heart leaps and she darts into the ladies room. Pulls from her pocket an untouched eight-ball of cocaine. She doesn't want to think about how she made it through security with that burning a hole in her pocket. But she is so glad to have it.

It's quarter to twelve when she does her first bump right there in the airport.

Outside the hospital she stands in the crusted snow and chain-smokes cigarettes. Her favorite cousin comes out to join her.

'Yo Mary. You made it.'

Jeremiah has red hair and freckles, he's six years her junior. Kicked out of Harvard for smoking weed, so they share a common bond.

'Jeremiah. What's up.' Mary lights her fourth cigarette since she's been standing out there. It's bitterly cold, but the shivering that wracks her body is entirely drug-induced.

'Sorry about your dad.'

'Yea.'

Mary hasn't cried yet - the cocaine nipped that in the bud.

'You in New York?'

'Yup.'

'Cool.'

They stand in silence for a bit, smoking. Then Mary remembers what she wants to ask him.

'So where's this place we're all staying?'

'Oh, uh, yea. Some friend of Uncle George's. Loaned us the house for everyone to crash.'

'So the whole family's staying together under one roof? Jesus.'

'Yea, but- '

'Not sure I can handle that.'

'Yea - but Mary-'

'Yea?'

'You're not.'

'What?'

'Um, I'm pretty sure your mother got you a hotel room in town.'

'What?'

'Yea.'

Mary should be relieved, but she's crushed, she's reeling.

'Sorry Mary, I thought you knew.'

'That's okay.'

'I don't know why your mother gives you such a bad rap.'

'Whatever.' Mary drops her cigarette in the snow, where it smolders briefly before going out. She steps on it anyway. 'Let's go inside. I'm freezing my ass off.'

After the service Mary is doing lines in the ladies room when her mother walks in. She's locked in the stall, but still, she's the only one in there and midway through a very large sniff. Her mother remains at the sink when Mary comes out. Just stands there, staring at Mary through the mirror as she washes her hands. Neither of them says anything. Mary doesn't need to look to see the tears streaming down her mother's face. She sighs, and with her hands still wet, she turns and takes her mother in her arms. They stay that way, holding each other, for a very long time.

The Carlsburg is empty. It won't fit in the pocket of the seat in front of her and Mary doesn't want to just put it on the floor. The train is humming along. Watching the fields, the houses, the back-ends of shopping centers whizzing by, Mary imagines her life, her past, the thoughts that won't stop banging around inside her head spilling out the window.

Her stomach is a mass of energy. Checks the time. 3:10. She's due to arrive in Manchester in less than twenty minutes. The man with the cart is making his way back through the train. Hands him her empty Carlsburg when he passes. Does not order another.

Her feet have started to wiggle. 'Happy feet,' her father used to call them. She's having trouble containing herself.

Outside it is overcast, threatening to drizzle.

2.

'Happy Birthday' is the title of the first message Jake ever sends her. Mary finds it the day she wakes up in bed with Guinevere and Nigel. Topless, sandwiched between them.

'Oh dear,' says Nigel, lifting the sheet just enough to see beneath it.

Mary, still half drunk, giggles and worms her way out. 'Sorry about that.' Scans the room for a scrap of clothing to cover herself. Finds a towel. 'I'll leave you two to it.'

Guinevere winks, puts a hand on Nigel's as he goes to reach for his spectacles. 'Not yet,' she says.

Mary closes the door, tiptoes through the hall to the bathroom. Sits on the toilet and stares at a black and white postcard taped to the wall - the Waterloo Bridge.

Remembers scraps from the night before - her birthday celebrations at the poetry open mike on Brick Lane. The endless gin and tonics with Guinevere. Nigel onstage, sawing his wrist, blood spurting everywhere - part of his act. The crowd going wild. The young poets she kissed - and the accordion player. The blurred late-night pub-crawl, the reckless cab ride home, the last fag in the garden. Getting it on with Carlos on the couch.

Upstairs, Carlos snores softly, right where she left him. Mary knows she's met him once before, though she's not sure when. He's Guinevere's old friend - the one who's crazy and well-read. An irresistible combination.

Remembers them kissing. Remembers sitting astride him. Not sure they didn't have sex. Spots her pink pants near the armrest, her red dress crumpled under his foot. Even as she approaches and reclaims her clothes, Carlos doesn't budge. Shimmies into the jeans and shakes out the dress - it's crusted with bits of tomato down the front so she brings it to the sink.

'You making tea?' asks Carlos. Now he is awake.

Mary turns, an arm across her breasts. 'Carlos.'

'What time is it?'

'Early. Sure you want to get up?'

Carlos waves his hand like it doesn't matter. 'Come over here.' Pats the space beside him without taking his eyes off her. 'Come.'

Mary is drawn to him even as the kettle begins to boil. Lies down in his arms. Just needs to press warm skin on skin - to soothe and even forget for just a few minutes the anxiety rising inside her.

Across the room she can see Guinevere's computer, thinks of the work she has to do. The editing deadlines looming. One order is due by three o'clock that afternoon - what time is it now?

Carlos runs his fingers over her back, tickles her spine right up under her hair. Rubs in tiny circles, so her body all the way down to the palms of her feet opens like a snail surging from its shell.

She almost kisses him, but the kettle is rocking hard now, screaming - like it might leap off the stove. Mary pecks him on the nose then extricates herself. Turns off the burner and takes her dress from the chair - it's still damp in front where she's rinsed it. She slips it back on. Finds two mugs and turns to Carlos, 'Tea?'

'Yes darling, please.' He says it cheerfully, even though his eyes are closed, hands clasped across his sternum.

Like a body laid to rest, she thinks.

Makes his tea the way she takes it herself - dark, extra-sweet. Brings it to him in the lounge.

'Ta,' he says, opening his eyes, sitting up.

'No problemo.' She's perched beside him, on the edge of the couch. They sip in silence.

After a bit, Mary puts her tea down on the floor and fetches Guinevere's computer. 'Okay, you have to help me with this.'

Carlos raises an eyebrow, says nothing.

Mary's logged into her work control panel, reads off the screen.

> Just as the famous detective Sherlock Holmes, I am always keen to look for evidence. What extremely fascinates me is the ability to uncover the tiny clues of a crime. Since I entered the high school, I had concentrated on figuring out the Chemical problems. By collecting useful information, I could make logical deductions, what was as detectives did. Due to my great effort, I won the First Prize in Chinese National Chemistry Olympiad during high school.

'What - the - fuck?' says Carlos.

'So cute.'

'Sherlock Holmes?'

'I love this kid.' Mary doesn't look up. She's focused on the essay, typing.

Carlos frees a hand, runs his finger along her lower back, where the flesh is exposed.

'Dude,' she says, brushing his hand away.

Carlos leans back and closes his eyes. Mary glances at him, then gets up. Carries the computer to the kitchen table where she clears a space amongst the mugs, dirty plates, ashtrays and crumpled cigarette packs.

Takes a deep breath. Two years on the job has taught her to suck it up - taught her the value of feigning confidence in the face of sheer panic. But until an order is completed, it's hard to fully relax. When several orders are outstanding, the pressure, for her, is relentless. Yet also addictive. The stress is a drug - best of all, it keeps her drinking fresh - a joy, as much as she has trouble controlling it.

Somewhere behind her, Guinevere's cat Monkey is mewing. Mary spots him, just outside the kitchen window. Where beams of sunlight are beginning to break through the canopy of trees in the garden.

Mary decides to give herself ten-minutes' leave of the Sherlock Holmes essay. Logs into Yahoo, Myspace - and that's when she finds it.

The message from Jake.

> Hello Mary,
>
> Happy Birthday!
>
> We don't really know each other, but it seems we are Myspace friends. So I thought I'd reach out and say hello, introduce myself.
>
> (In truth, ever since I read your one-acts in the 'New Voices' anthology I have felt compelled to write you...)

Mary's breath catches, the world around her freezes to a halt. She continues to read.

> (If it mitigates the freak-factor any, I am a friend of Roger Trumbull's - I believe he was in the same graduate playwriting program as you at UCL? maybe a year or two ahead. Perhaps you two know each other?)

'Holy crap.' She looks over her shoulder, checks out Carlos on the couch. He's lying still - she can't see his face but judging by his breathing he might well be asleep.

> ...I simply wanted to say I greatly enjoyed your work.
>
> (especially the piece with the dog monologue. I may ask your permission to perform it at a later date. I myself am a sometimes-actor and most-of-the-time poet:-)
>
> Best,
> Jake T. Potter

Mary sits there and stares. Reads the message again. It's the PS that gets her - and gives him away.

> PS Your smile. You do know how amazing it is, right? (I'm sure people must tell you all the time!) Anyway, for days now it's been stuck in my mind.

'Oh my God,' Mary whispers. 'Oh my God oh my God.'

The fantasy begins as she's taking a shower. Does not involve anything concrete or domestic. Has no specific parameters. Is more a sense, a warm safe feeling, like soft breath just behind her ear.

With the water spraying over her, shampoo in her eyes - she's not worrying about her edits, she's thinking about Jake. His photo on Myspace is slightly distorted, in black and white. Lends him an old-fashioned quality. Makes her think of Steve McQueen. Pale eyes and fair - his hair might be ginger or blonde. She pictures strong hands.

Standing there, enveloped in steam, she doesn't notice the door to the bathroom opening, Carlos slipping in. But when he steps in behind her and fits his body right up against hers she does not move away or even flinch. He kisses her back, his lips move along the curve of her shoulder, up towards the nape of her neck. A rush of warmth spreads out from her pelvis. Still she doesn't move. Carlos stiffens, presses into her, and she is torn - to get out, or turn around and open herself. To kiss him hard and feel his tongue wet and thick against hers.

Mary turns. She would be facing him, except she's looking down. 'I'm sorry,' she says.

Carlos doesn't say anything. Is neither disappointed nor surprised. Merely gives her a wry smile. A rivulet of water dashes across his face, from just above his right temple straight down to his chin. Before she climbs out, he slips a hand between her legs. Drags his fingertips up to her belly, then cups each breast.

Back in the kitchen, wrapped in a towel with Guinevere's computer under one arm, Mary opens the back door and drifts out to the garden. Monkey is at the top of the fence.

She takes a seat on the bench, opens the computer, and gazes at Jake's message, his tiny vague photo.

'Jesus.'

Tilts the screen to keep the words visible with each shift in the sun. All she can think of is this is her birthday gift from the universe. Reads and rereads it, until the words on the screen double and blur.

'Fuck.'

'What is it?' Guinevere thuds through the kitchen and out the French doors. Her blonde hair is all tangled, so much pale flesh exposed, the way her oversized jumper hangs off her.

Nigel lingers in the doorway. Minus his spectacles, he looks sheepish and pale.

'Check it out,' says Mary.

'Let's see.' Guinevere takes a seat beside her. Her body is supple and warm, reeks of sex. Pulls a pair of red-framed glasses from her cleavage, then squints at the screen. 'What am I looking at darling?'

'A message. On Myspace.'

'Okay…'

Mary is up, pacing. 'I need a cigarette.'

'Bloody hell, chicken!' Guinevere exclaims as she reads.

'I know.'

'Wait - look at this-'

'I know,' Mary shudders.

'Hold on,' says Guinevere. 'Let me read it again.'

A kettle trills. Nigel has disappeared back inside.

'Sweetheart, this is fantastic.'

'Yea?' Mary lights a cigarette and hands it to Guinevere. Lights herself another. The two of them smoke.

'He's fucking gorgeous!' Guinevere says, exhaling. 'Jake. The sometimes actor. The poet. I love it!'

'It's weird.'

'He likes your smile - he wants you.'

'Scary.'

'It's cool.'

'Whatever.'

'What are you going to do?'

'I dunno,' says Mary. 'Go home and go to sleep?'

'No, but what are you going to do?'

Nigel giggles. He's back in the doorway, cradling a cup of tea in his slender hands. 'She has an admirer.' He says it out loud - not as a question, just a simple statement. Then he says, 'Jake the Stranger. Woo-woo!'

'Woo-woo,' Guinevere echoes.

They all giggle. Mary blushes.

'Okay,' Guinevere stands up to leave. 'I'm going to shower.'

Once she's gone, Mary lies down on the bench beneath the lilacs and snapdragons. Closes her eyes and lets out a breath. Listens to the rustling of the leaves. An airplane passes overhead. Music wafts from an upstairs flat.

Jake's face fills her mind's eye. She lies perfectly still. Only her eyelids are flickering.

Walking home that day she nearly gets hit by a bus. She's so busy in her head composing a reply to Jake - telling him she's so pleased to meet him. She doesn't look up. Starts to cross at an intersection, her eyes on the pavement. When the bus stops, her face is only inches from its seams. A fellow pedestrian - a woman not much older than she is - stares at her stunned.

'You almost got hit.'

Not an accusation - she says it out of wonder. Still, Mary is embarrassed, looks down at her Converse.

Approaching Upper Street in Islington she spots a Sainsbury's on the corner. Her stomach is roiling. Ploughman's pickle might be nice. Yes, she thinks, God bless this country, especially for the sandwiches - a poor girl's salvation and delight. In every supermarket, corner store, petrol station, newsstand - so many lovely sandwiches to be had, and all of them so cheap.

Hands in pockets, sweating, she strides along the high road, passing Starbucks, pubs and café's. Passing Angel Tube. Nearly to Spitalfields. Feels like it's been hours since she left Stoke Newington.

She keeps walking. At dusk she's near the turreted flat she shares in Leicester Square. But she keeps going - through the back alleys of Soho, then Chinatown to the Strand. Down to the river, where she crosses at Embankment.

In the fading sun everything glows and casts a shadow - the water is luminous pink. All along the bridge, groups of tourists pose for photographs before the spectacular sky.

Mary closes her eyes and leans over the rail. Lets the wind whip her hair in her face. Makes herself dizzy imagining she's about to fall, all the way down.

Stepping off the bridge onto the South Bank, it's properly dark out. She walks right into Royal Festival Hall and heads straight for the stairs. On the upper level, just outside the Skylon Restaurant, she stands flush against the plate-glass windows, looking out at the river and the City of London - it's breathtaking, all glittering at night like some sprawling carnival.

Men and women in suits and cocktail dresses walk past, making their way into dinner. Mary watches as they are met by elegant male hostesses and escorted to their tables. She imagines coming to this restaurant with her father; it seems like a distant possibility, something she might have done in a different life. One very far from the one she's living now.

3.

From: Mary Cartwright <scarymary666@yahoo.com>
To: jakepverse@hotmail.com
Subject: re: smiler
Date: Mon, 18 Sept 2006 11:11 am

I am glad you too think it is kind of a fantastic thing, this acquaintance...
I am smiling a bit more on my travels. in fact some dude said "beautiful smile" as I sped past him on my way to this here starshmucks. and I was not even aware that I was smiling. But I was pondering you...

***

'Wait, how long has it been?' asks Vanessa.

They are at an AT&T Wireless shop in Knightsbridge, buying Mary a cell phone. Her old one was lost on her birthday night out. Only now, nearly three weeks later, Vanessa has offered to buy her a new one.

'Um, how long?' Mary is stalling. Normally she tells Vanessa everything, tells her the truth. But the speed with which she's become besotted with Jake is startling, even by her standards. 'A few weeks,' she says. 'But they've been intense, incredible.'

'Mm,' says Vanessa, pulling a pink Motorola off the shelf. 'You know when it's right, I guess, don't you? What do you think of this one?'

'Let me see!' pipes up June, Vanessa's six-year-old daughter. Conceived in Soho House during a one-night stand and the motivating force behind Vanessa's spectacular rise in finance.

'Careful.' Vanessa gives her the phone. 'It's your favorite color, isn't it June-bug?'

'Yes.'

'Mine too,' says Mary.

June giggles. 'Here Mummy, Mary would like to have this one.'

'I can get it V, really. You've helped me out enough. What is it? Twenty pounds or something?'

'Thirty-nine.' Vanessa is pulling out her wallet, waves Mary away. 'Out of your budget, really, let me, I don't mind.'

'Let Mummy, Mary,' June echoes.

'Oh jeeze.' Mary wilts, unable to look either of them in the eye. Until her next paycheck she has only thirty pounds to her name. And after nearly three weeks of using only email to reach people, having a phone again will be nice.

Really she's only thinking in terms of Jake. Now she'll be ready for when they exchange numbers.

The three of them paused out in front of the store. Mary uncomfortable, never sure how to part gracefully, say goodbye. It's a Sunday afternoon and the Kensington High Street is flush with shoppers, but lazy ones. Traffic on the sidewalks and in the streets lacks the urgency and aggression of a weekday.

Late September, and even at close to half five, it might be more than sixty degrees, the breeze spongy and warm.

Vanessa's hair is peroxided to a glossy bone color and scraped back. Her face has such delicate features. She scrutinizes Mary like a mother does her favorite, most difficult child.

'Hey, how would you like to housesit for my coworker? He's off to Indonesia for three weeks at the end of October. Has the most wretched little dog.'

'Oh my God, totally. I'm there.'

'I'll see what I can do. Get you out of that cesspool in Leicester Square for a bit.'

'It's not so bad.'

'Mary. So where you off to? Come have Sunday dinner with us.'

'Oh V. I can't. I have a ton of work. I should get back.'

'Nonsense,' says Vanessa. 'I insist.'

'Mummy, is Mary having with supper with us?' June stares up at her mother, solemn as a chorus girl.

'Would you like that June?' says Mary.

'Ye-es,' says June, still staring at her mother.

Vanessa winks at Mary. 'We need to pick up a few things first.'

At the Waitrose on the corner Vanessa buys salmon fillets, yogurt, grapes, fresh vegetables - not only asparagus for steaming, but also the fixings for a salad. Plus goat cheese and brie, two boxes of cereal, ice cream and two bottles of red wine. The wine is expensive - nearly twenty pounds apiece - a far cry from Mary's old stand-by, Jacob's Creek.

By normal standards it's a modest haul, but Mary's been scraping by for so long she can't help fantasizing what it would be like to shop like this on a daily basis.

They make their way slowly up the Campden Hill Road to Vanessa's luxury loft-condominium. June and Mary lag a few feet behind so they can sneak grapes from the bag June is carrying.

'Okay,' says Vanessa, the minute they are through her door. 'Mary, use that laptop on the kitchen table. I want to see some pictures of this Jake.'

So as June puts away groceries and Vanessa prepares their meal, Mary reads aloud Jake's emails, points out his Myspace photo.

'My God, he looks just like Steve McQueen!' Vanessa exclaims when she sees it.

'I know, that's what I thought. Hold on, look at this one...'

Through a simple Google image search Mary finds his picture three other places. One is next to his bio, where a poem of his has been published online. Another is a cast photo, from a play at the Exchange. The third is Jake in a pub - from an online photo album related to a theater company he's been involved with, 'The Revolutionaries.'

'My God. He's so hot,' Vanessa whispers.

'I know, right?'

'He chose you. That's good. Read me some of his emails again. I think you should to hang on to this one.'

From: jakepverse@hotmail.com
To: scarymary666@yahoo.com
Subject: not the least contrary…
Date: Tue, 26 Sept 2006 1:19 pm

Mary Mary...

Are you working on your edits? Snuggled in some hectic London café, in a corner, banging away at your laptop? That is how I am picturing you now. To answer your question, indeed, I have thought often about moving to London. Most of the action is there (theatrically speaking at least, probably poetically as well.) I guess I always assumed I would wind up there eventually. But circumstances have continued to crop up that keep me in Manchester. Now my state of affairs is such that I'm fairly rooted to this place (am I being too vague? my apologies if I am - it's one of my strengths I'm afraid.) But enough about me! I want to know more about you - your likes and dislikes, your favorite films - and plays! I meant it when I said I would love permission to do some of your work! Lately I've been reading a great deal of Beckett- not just plays - today it's Malloy (perched here in the kitchen with a cup of split pea soup & me mittens on!) This morning had a lovely walk in the park (yikes!! am I boring you to tears? this is what happens when a man has too much time in excess alone. I should stop.) Oh Mary, sweet Mary - I would like to walk with you. I imagined as much...

***

Not long after Vanessa buys her the pink phone, around the time of her lunch with Uncle George, Mary decides to make the trip up to Manchester to meet Jake once and for all. He hasn't invited her - hasn't even suggested it. But already he feels like her boyfriend, her soul mate even. Mary can't wait around any more.

From: scarymary666@yahoo.com
To: jakepverse@hotmail.com
Subject: perhaps?
Date: Mon, 2 Oct 2006 2:56 pm

Jake,

I may actually be in Manchester in a week or so - and of course I would love to meet up - perhaps you could show me around? If you are not too embarrassed to be seen with a retardo Americano, that is. Okay, so we may have to get stinking drunk...

When he doesn't respond right away she begins to panic - the thought even crosses her mind he might have another girlfriend. But he doesn't let her down.

From: jakepverse@hotmail.com
To: scarymary666@yahoo.com
Subject: re: perhaps?
Date: Tues, 3 Oct 2006 9:29 am

Darling,

I am excited you are coming! But are you sure you want to venture this far north? It's frightfully cold and usually raining- I have to be honest, I'm worried you'll be bored & I won't be able to show you a good time.

It's been awhile since I had a new friend...

***

No one would believe by the way she conducts herself - all plucky adventurer and reckless nomad - that she is actually a little bit scared. Something about Manchester as a city seems particularly feral and dangerous. She imagines great industrial red brick buildings and desolate streets. Drizzle and big gusts of wind. Karl Marx and football thugs. Posses of Morrissey boys in combat boots and quiffs lingering about the YMCAs and cemeteries.

The combination of brutal elements, physical danger, Communism and disaffected sadness scares the living daylights out of her.

But she goes ahead with her plans. Books a cheap hotel room and train tickets. Takes on extra editing orders so she is working around the clock, sleeping only two or three hours to meet all her deadlines. There is no internet in the flat she shares in Leicester Square, so she creeps out at dawn, hurrying through the back alleys of Chinatown to the twenty-four hour net-café. Amidst the drunks and club kids slumped at the other computers, she pops in her memory stick and uploads all her orders.

High on lack of sleep and the satisfaction of a grueling job completed just in time, she wanders back up the Charing Cross Road, debating how she might indulge herself for her efforts - a splurge on an extra strong mocha and almond croissant at the Pret-a-Manger on the corner? Or a visit to the Oasis Leisure Centre and their glorious year-round heated outdoor pool?

She waits, so she can go to the pool at night. With the lights from the tall buildings reflecting on the water, everything is cast in so many exhilarating shades of blue. All lit up, in the center of Covent Garden, she floats on her back in the dark and gazes up at the sky. In these moments, there is no other place she would rather be - not out in the pub with the rest of London, not even with Jake. If any of them knew what they were missing at night in the pool - it is magic.

Later, after she showers and gets dressed and blow-dries her hair, she savors the anticipation of Jake's last email of the day - without fail, he now sends her one last message sometime in the evening.

From: jakepverse@hotmail.com
To: Mary Cartwright <scarymary666@yahoo.com>
Subject: wings of desire
Date: Thur, 5 Oct 2006 8:55 pm

sweetheart. hope your day went well. watch the Wim Wenders film on ITV tonight - it's one of my favorites...

From: jakepverse@hotmail.com
To: Mary Cartwright <scarymary666@yahoo.com>
Subject: Be Forewarned
Date: Fri, 6 Oct 2006 6:49 pm

Pretty one. I am so tired. Alas, must raise myself from the dead for a theater company fundraiser tonight (so the Revolutionaries can continue to fight the good fight!) Yours truly will be performing a scene from Pinter for the Manchester deep pockets. Wish me luck!

(Strong chance I will write you drunk later...)

From: jakepverse@hotmail.com
To: Mary Cartwright <scarymary666@yahoo.com>
Subject: my minx
Date: Mon, 9 Oct 2006 9:44 pm

Darling,

Were you teasing me when you said you swam in pigtails and a bikini? Well. I am a cad. It got me through the day...

'Manchester Piccadilly,' the conductor says, an awkward momentum propelling him forward as the train brakes into its berth. He's flushed, stubble showing. Pulls ticket stubs from the top of each seat as he goes.

Mary slings her knapsack over her shoulder, grabs her canvas book bag. The others in her car - mainly business types in modest suits - fold away their laptops, wrestle with the flaps, zips and buckles of their attaché cases.

Now they are in the station, the windows are dark. Mary can see the tiniest details in her reflection - the creases around her eyes, the birthmark on her neck. Who was it that said birthmarks were left over from a past life? Now she can't stop theorizing what was there - a bullet hole? A finger print? A kiss?

Stepping off the train she's hit with a blast of cold and stops short. Just to stand there, caught in the current of so many people, fills her with hope. Stares up at the airy domed roof, her chest expanding to match the vast latticework of steel beams crisscrossed above. All the railway stations of Europe like giant greenhouses.

She parks herself by the WH Smith's. Stands there like she's examining the arrivals and departures board. Every thirty seconds it changes, the names of towns flipping over on themselves like rows of Dominos. She's grappling for her bearings, trying not to appear like she's seeing everything for the very first time. Like she knows which exit to take.

On an upper level there's an O'Neill's Pub, and already at half three in the afternoon there's a healthy crowd. Others sitting, smoking, at the dingy plastic tables just outside. So many bald men with ruddy faces, broad chests and glinting eyes.

Northern accents so strong they might be speaking another language.

Outside it's already getting dark. She's reluctant to leave the station, even though she's staked out her hotel on the map. She's chosen the Britannia not only for its cheap rooms - it should be just around the corner.

Mary shifts her knapsack, feels for her wallet, her cell phone. Walks clear across the station, and out the large set of sliding glass doors. To her right is an arcade of shops, to her left what looks to be a main road with a tram line. The wind has kicked up, so she ducks over to a stoop just outside a greasy spoon to light her cigarette. Holds it up near her face, taking quick deep drags, enjoying the here and the now. People filtering past, the occasional tram, the sky cresting - now a soot-tinged peach.

At last, she thinks.

Before her cigarette is done, she sets off. Sees the Britannia when she reaches the first intersection. A banner suspended from an upper story flutters in the wind. Rooms £39 per night.

The single they give her is the size of a stall, with one window and a tiny skylight. First she strips off her jeans. Lights a cigarette. Pokes her head in the bathroom, gives the bed a sit-bounce. Opens the closet.

The heat is blasting and after a few uninspired tugs at the window, she climbs on a table and manages to pry open the skylight a crack. Hops down, stubs out her cigarette. Investigates the tea tray. Eats both packets of complimentary biscuits standing in front of the mirror.

Lights another cigarette. Takes a seat at the vanity and sets up her laptop. Smiles. Jake is waiting for her in her inbox.

From: jakepverse@hotmail.com

To: Mary Cartwright <scarymary@yahoo.com>
Subject: re: see you soon☺
Date: Fri, 13 Oct 2006 2:25 pm

Darling,

Are you really coming to Manchester tomorrow!? I can hardly believe it. Mary, I must be honest. I'm actually a little anxious about showing you interesting things to do-

(Unless you count whiling away the hours in a pub watching Man City get trounced by Sheffield United as a suitable pastime? That's usually how I spend my Saturday afternoons.)

Although I was thinking in honor of your visit we could do something cultural - maybe check out a museum or go see a film. Do you like doing those things Mary? Funny, I feel like I know you and yet I know nothing about you...

He leaves his number.

Btw, I'm at 0798 556 789. So you have it. xxjtp

He has no idea she's already there. It's delicious.

***

Walking into the wind along Portland Street. Bound for the Tesco's she remembers seeing on her way from the train. It's dark out, and she needs to buy cigarettes and wine. Knows at Tesco's it will be cheaper.

She's not wearing a hat and her ears sting. The cold is serious, chimes in with her fear.

Sees the Tesco's up ahead two more blocks. She's stopped at a red light, a tram coming so she can't just dash across, has to wait. Eyes the group of men approaching, only a few feet away - thick-set football fans in work boots and bright red Manchester United jerseys. Two are bald and the third has dreadlocks. All of them drinking from enormous cans of lager.

Mary looks down. They are beside her now - she smells the liquor on their breath, their body odor like onions.

Just as she senses their gazes upon her the light changes. Breaks into a run like she has to get somewhere, she's late - not like she's fleeing from them. Trips crossing the broken pavement near the tracks, but keeps going, too spooked to look back. Doesn't stop until she's standing in front of the Tesco's, safe in the fluorescent glow of its windows.

Catches her breath. She's nauseas but still she reaches in her pocket for her cigarettes. Lights up and smokes quickly.

Entering the store, she's in the sandwich section. Goes for an egg and cress. Considers one of the salads as well - tuna and sweet corn made with lumps of mayo - decides not. They also cost more. All she's eaten that day is an almond croissant from the Pret-a-Manger in Leicester Square.

The market bustles with university students. Chatting, laughing all around her. Save for a word to the train conductor, and a few more to the friendly young man at the Britannia front desk, Mary's had another one of those days where she hasn't really spoken to anyone.

At the wine aisle now, red or white? She wants both, but she's only going to allow herself one - for her there's no such thing as 'stocking up.' Settles for a bottle of red with a screw top because in the end, she truly believes white wine is for pussies.

In the checkout line one of her eyelids starts to twitch. Stares down at the linoleum-tiled floor - someone has spilled pumpkin seeds all over. Nudges them into a mound with her toe. Soon she's at the register, asking for cigarettes, stuffing everything in a plastic bag, hurrying out into the night.

Now the streets are thronging with what seem like roving bands of Vikings. The football match has ended and enormous men are congregated on every street corner, in front of every bar. It's terrifying - the air is vicious and alive - every shout, every unidentified slam and siren might be coming from a fight. Someone getting their face kicked-in, someone getting knifed. Mary runs the whole way back to the Britannia, the violence of the entire country chasing at her heels.

Safe in her room, she uncaps the wine. Tells herself just one glass, and no more. Not until she's checked her work emails, polished off the day's edits, responded to clients.

> Subject: From Youngsam -Thank you
> From: "Youngsam" <youngsam326@yahoo.com.cn>
> Date: Fri, October 13, 2006 7:36 pm
> To: mary_cartwright@editpro.com
>
> Dear Mary,
>
> Thank you for your kind and detailed corrections. Although you might say it is just doing your job, it also really sends your warm heart through this logic-based data structure which will never be like yours.
>
> I appreciate it and want to send you back with my pray that God be with you(I will also be sorry if you are uncomfortable with Christianity).
>
> I just a little worried about you, for you usually work all night. Keep healthy!
>
> Have a nice day. Best wishes,
>
> Youngsam.

At half nine she shuts down her computer, tops up her glass. Notices the bottle is now less than half full. Wishes she'd bought two.

Twenty minutes later the wine is gone. Mary gets up from the vanity, finds her jeans, puts on lipstick, runs her hands through her hair and leaves the smoky cocoon of her room.

Walks into the Britannia bar just in time to catch the ten o'clock news. The place is empty save for two businessmen and the bartender. Oasis is playing but she can still hear the TV. The US is killing civilians, and Bush is sending more troops. Earthquakes in China and floods in Indonesia. Employment is down, and bank rates are on the rise.

The bartender fixes her with a smile. 'What'll it be?'

Mary pauses to consider. 'Hmmm.' Lights a cigarette. Really she knows. 'A glass of Merlot, please.'

'So you American then?' He pours her a glass, a large one.

'How'd you guess?' she giggles. Hands him a tenner. He might be in his mid-twenties Mary decides. Has one of those spiky short haircuts so prevalent in England. His hair is the color of Vanessa's - but his is not dyed.

'So where you from in the States?'

'Well,' Mary weighs what to tell him. Since her father died she has a mental block when it comes to thinking of anyplace as home. There's Boston and Washington DC where her parents divided their time when she was growing up, and New York City, where she's spent most of her adult life. She opts for New York - everyone knows it, wants to go there.

'I been there once, it's right crowded, yeah? So many bars. Went to the top of the Empire State. That was scary as fuck!'

'Yea, you know, all my years there, I've never done that.'

'You should go, it's well worth it. You afraid of heights?'

'Definitely.'

'I'm Nick by the way.' He wipes his hand on the cloth at his belt, then offers it to her.

'Mary.'

'Mary. What brings you to Manchester, Mary?'

Her wine is nearly done, and the room is starting to tip ever so slightly. She needs food, but she's too shy to ask for nuts. 'Oh, ah - doing some research.'

'Research? What, you a scientist?'

'No, no. Um, I write plays.'

'No kidding?' Nick says, breaking into a grin. 'So you writing about Manchester then? Oh, hey - another Merlot?' He nods towards Mary's empty glass.

'Ah, no that's okay.' She slides from her stool. 'I think I'm going to head up.'

'Right then. Nice to meet you Mary-' Nick waves after her and Mary manages what she hopes is a casual smile.

'You too Nick.'

Really her face feels like it's caving in - the glass of Merlot has pushed her over the edge. Takes the elevator to her floor, glad she meets nobody in the hall. Her head so thick she might be a gargoyle.

Back in her room, she eats the sandwich she bought at Tesco's. Egg and cress, several hours warm.

5.

Wakes at nine in a panic. First thought is how much did she have to drink the night before? Starts counting them down in her head: glass of Merlot at the bar, bottle of wine in her room, Carlsburg on the train. Not so bad - she feels better. Second thought is Jake. Today they are meeting up! And she never responded to his email...

Next she thinks of the three edits she still has to finish.

Gets up from the bed, turns on the electric kettle, goes to the loo. Makes instant coffee mixed with an entire packet of cocoa. Lights a cigarette, resumes her perch at the vanity and opens her computer.

> From: Mary Cartwright <scarymary666@yahoo.com>
> To: jakepverse@hotmail.com
> Subject: today
> Date: Sat, 14 Oct 2006 9:17 am
>
> Dear Jake,
>
> Northward-bound! Should arrive sometime before 1pm. Happy to meet up with you whenever - or not (if something has come up or you change your mind - it's okay, really! I'm cool either way☺
>
> Oh - and so you have it, my mobile is 0777 683 4559…

Happy Feet under the desk. Now he has her number, he could text her. At any moment.

She works through the morning, her phone out. Volume on. Checks her email at noon. Nothing. Tells herself it's still early yet. Decides to head out for a walk.

Cuts up through Chinatown to Deansgate. In daylight, the city is subdued. She finds a Pret and stops for a mocha. Savors it, seated on a high stool by the window where she can watch the people passing by. Her phone is out, next to her coffee cup.

Someone has left behind *The Independent* and she flips through it, scanning the sports section for the times of the football matches. Manchester City plays at three.

Walks towards the Arndale Center, then turns around, rebuffed by the growing crowds. Along Corporation Street she comes upon several tourists gathered at a simple postbox. Mary is curious and joins them. Reads on a plaque:

> This postbox remained standing almost undamaged on June 18th 1996 when this area was devastated by a bomb. The box was removed during the rebuilding of the city centre and was returned to its original site on November 22nd 1999.

She walks on, ends up back where she was earlier along Deansgate. Keeps going until she is standing in a large square, staring up at the Town Hall. Like something out of the Victorian novels she devoured as an English major in college.

By now she's carrying on a conversation with Jake in her head. Hears herself saying, 'Went for a walk by the Town Hall – it was amazing.'

No, she checks herself, horrified. She can't be as boring as that.

Lingers at the statue of Agricola – builder of 'the breast shaped hill' – the fortress Mamicam. Makes her way around until she comes to the library. Pictures Marx striding up the stairs, head down, beard out of control, wearing some kind of black overcoat.

Enters, and goes up floor by floor. The place is empty, warm – Mary revels in the smell of old books in crinkly protective wrappers, piles of them, in uneven rows on the beige metal stacks. Finds herself in Drama and Fiction near the top, where the air is driest. Trolls through the plays. An impressive selection of Sam Shepard. Pinter and Shakespeare, no Aphra Behn. In Fiction, checks for Rhys and Kavan; finds *Wide Sargasso Sea* and *Julia and the Bazooka*.

The time according to her phone is now three o'clock. Maybe once he's settled at the pub, she thinks, he'll text her to join him.

Half four and Mary is at the bar in the Britannia, buzzed after two glasses of red wine. The game is on, and it's a tie - not a single goal has been scored. The room is a sea of light blue jerseys, a Manchester City crowd. Mary's in awe and a little scared of the company she's in - but it makes for good, fierce drinking.

A part of her has accepted she won't be hearing from Jake. Maybe he's expecting her to call him? No, she decides. He has her number. He's the guy.

And strangely, it's okay - now she's started, she's primed to abandon all hope in favor of getting shitfaced drunk. She's tired, and the thought of meeting Jake after so much buildup is almost too much.

Six o'clock and the game ends in a draw - zero zero. Mary's back in her room. Has a change of heart. Starts getting dressed to go out. She's had enough to drink, she decides she will text Jake after all.

> Hey it's me:-) Fancy meeting up someplace around Portland Street?

Silence.

Then her phone beeps. Heart thudding she snaps it up, reads the message.

> The following errors occurred while sending and receiving messages: Your text message cannot be sent.

Mary is stunned. Then the ugly thought occurs to her. Something about the number he's given - the number of digits, specifically.

Opens her laptop and brings up his email. Checks the number again. Yes, that's it - it's short a digit.

'Fuck.'

Still, she reminds herself, he has her number.

'Fuck.'

Resaves his number as *JTP Maybe*.

Mary spends the next ten minutes lying on the bed meditating. Thinks on the numbers, *0798 556 789*. Maybe he left out a 9 - his number is probably 0798 556 7899!

Because she has nothing to lose, she sends a text to this number. It goes through. She waits.

Decides for good measure, to go ahead and text 7890, 7898, 7897 as well.

They all go through. She waits. At last her phone beeps - someone has texted her back! 7897. Again, her heart pounds as she opens the message.

> Who is this?

***

Half seven and Mary is back at the Britannia bar, fresh pack of Marlboros at her elbow.

Nick says, 'What'll it be New York?'

Fills her with pride. Barely twenty-four hours she's been there, already people know her. 'Glass of Merlot,' she says. Why not?

Half nine she's back in her room. On the bed, everything spinning - the dresser, the bureaus, the lamps. Falls asleep thinking what she really needs is some cocaine.

***

Date: Sun, 15 Oct 2006 9:46 am
From: 'Vanessa Hope-Jones'
Subject: house-sit!
To: 'Mary Cartwright'

Good news!

I told my coworker Aymerick what a fine upstanding citizen you are, and he would be thrilled to entrust you with the care of his home & two precious darlings, Jazzy the dog, and kitty Gaspard (oui oui, le garcon est Francais!)

Has a lovely little flat in Notting Hill, off the Pembridge Gardens. You will be able to visit me and Junie at will - it's just a skip & a jump!

Would start 31st October through November 16 - does that work for you? Have given him your number so he will be calling you directly to make arrangements.

Bisous!

Sunday. Mary confronts her emails, but there's no word from Jake. She can't bear to check out. Not yet. Calls down to the front desk and tells them she's staying another night. Spends the day working, nursing her hangover. Only when it's starting to get dark out does she get dressed. Heads down to the lobby, hands over more cash for her room.

This time she walks towards Oxford Street. Turns left and just keeps going - past the Cornerhouse, the University - it's getting darker and darker, she just keeps walking.

Oxford Street becomes Oxford Road, then she's on Wilmslow Road. Passing curry houses, Asian shops - the smells are spicy and rich - she's hungry but she hasn't brought her wallet. Windows filled with shiny purple beads, mylar streamers, red and green metallic decorations like it's Christmas in October.

Just as she's about to turn around she reaches Platt Fields Park. The gates are still open; she's scared but goes inside. Follows a path along the edge of the fields, then finds herself in a sparse wood. Still a few stray students out jogging, kids playing, their ball glowing white in the dusk.

Even with these others in sight, something feels ominous, not safe. Breaks into a jog when she can't find an exit. The wind has picked up.

Thinks she hears someone coming up behind her. In that split second the park seems to have emptied. Something catches her hair - she startles. It's nothing. A branch.

Now she sees the gate up ahead, beyond it the lights and the traffic. She's euphoric - grins against the cold air, her eyes watering, the city spread out before her.

That night, back in her silent room, she sits on the bed in her underwear and smokes. Through the gauze curtains, hovering low over the rooftops, a red-orange moon.

***

From: jakepverse@hotmail.com
To: Mary Cartwright <scarymary@yahoo.com>
Subject: did I miss you?
Date: Mon, 16 Oct 2006 9:31 am

Mary,

Oh no! I only just received the email you sent me on Saturday- was without internet for the weekend, else I would have called you (at least now I have your number☺ You did get my number, though, I emailed on fri?) I don't blame you for not wanting to hang out- hopefully you were up to something far more thrilling than watching Man City draw with Sheffield. When I didn't hear from you on Saturday I actually wound up calling it a night after the game & staying in.
(you see, I'm really quite a bore!)

But I do hope we can meet up soon! (either when you visit again, or if I am in London...) And I'm dying to hear all about your visit & what you thought of Manchester!

xoJTPxx

From: Mary Cartwright <scarymary666@yahoo.com>
To: jakepverse@hotmail.com
Subject: Re: did I miss you?
Date: Mon, 16 Oct 2006 9:47 am

Jake,

I'm still here.

***

Mary is lying face-up on the bed, staring at the ceiling. Wondering what it would be like if she could live in the Britannia Hotel forever. Smoking and writing, drinking tea in the daytime, and whiskey and wine at night. Subsisting on the complimentary biscuits housekeeping supplies with the tea bags and fresh sheets.

Her phone on the bedside table beeps.

Okay, how about half eight tonight at Fab Café?
We'll meet for sherry and narcotics JTPx

Mary notes the last four digits of his phone number are 7891.

Saves it as *JTP*.

Deletes the entry for *JTP Maybe*.

6.

From: Mary Cartwright <scarymary666@yahoo.com>
To: ladyguineveretoo@hotmail.com
Subject: sherry & narcotics
Date: Mon, 16 Oct 2006 1:15 pm

oh. My. God.
Call me at some point.

My phone is off as the battery is growing weak and I forgot my charger but if you can swing it I am ensconced in the Britannia hotel in Manchester 0161 228 2288 room 246.

I received a txt.

I get the sense that I am about to be SEVERELY corrupted. And educated.

Monday late afternoon. Jake's text fills Mary's head with fantasies of being tied up and ravaged. She's chain-smoking, unable to work, hopping around in her t-shirt and underpants. Like she's doing a rain dance around the unopened bottle of sherry that sits on the vanity in place of her computer. Buys it the minute she gets his text, the most expensive bottle in the store.

Because it's nearly dark out she decides it's okay to have some. Breaks the seal and pours herself a glass, checking her eyes in the mirror to make sure she looks okay. Looks normal. Not like she's been holed up in a hotel room for the better part of three days.

***

Two hours later, it's 7:45. She's showered and dressed, her face flushed. Wears what she always does when she needs to look good -

it's all she has - the red spaghetti strap dress over her favorite pink jeans.

The bottle of sherry has a huge dent in it and she's starting to see things like some kind of montage: her toiletries spread out in the over-bright bathroom, the dim lamp on the dresser, jeans strewn across the floor, through the drapes the blurred lights of the city below.

Mary grabs her phone, keycard, lipstick, wallet and Marlboros. Steps into the hall. Walks right past the elevator, takes the grand circular staircase. In her head she's Cinderella, gliding beneath the chandeliers, a hand on the shiny brass rail.

At the bottom she pauses. The lobby is thronging with bleached-blonde bridesmaids in pastel dresses and beaming, red-faced groomsmen in matching cummerbunds. Standing by the banister, swaying slightly, she even spots the bride and groom.

Peers through the bar to the banquet hall, where a DJ is playing Girls Aloud to a handful of children and grandparents. Most of the wedding party is packed in the bar, watching Liverpool play Arsenal. 'Oohing' and 'aaahing' with each near miss and save.

Nick winks to her from across the room and she wants to wink back but she's had way too much sherry. Instead she nods and tries to make her way forward without seeming to weave or wobble. At this particular stage in her drinking - drunk, but not yet wasted - self-consciousness has the effect of making her seem even more sloshed than she is.

So it's a relief when she steps outside and not only is it freezing, it's pitch black. Her impulse is to wander, to take out more cash, buy candy or a pack of gum. But really there is no avoiding it. It's time to meet Jake.

At first it's so dark when she enters the bar she can't make out anyone. The walk in the cold has sobered her. She's caught in that terrifying exposed place where she knows people can see her while she is helpless to hide or blend in. Every nerve in her body is rattled and screaming to flee, to turn right back around and bolt into the night. She pictures her little hotel room, the bottle of sherry on the bedside table. Pictures herself in her underwear, perched on top of the covers, chain-smoking cigarettes and watching TV.

Jake!

Sees him now, and he sees her too. He is smiling and waving - then both of them, shy, looking down.

His hair is flaming wild - a great quiff of crimson, like some spectacular twentieth century 'Archie.' But his features are delicate, almost feminine. Blue, blue, eyes - in the darkness they almost glow white.

Her first thought is he is far too good-looking for her. Feels his eyes on her as she makes her way across the room. Now she's clumsy, like a little kid.

'Mary? Mary is it, yeah?'

'Yea - Jake? Hey.'

Everything is swirling, twirling. They might be on a carnival teacup ride, the room whipping past. The space between them, the only part that's still. Two strangers who have exchanged intimacies but never met - not sure whether to hug or kiss - or simply shake.

They wind up doing all three. Jake grabs her hand, she goes in for a hug. They kiss somewhere near each other's earlobes. Mary gets a strong whiff of a clean lemony scent - that and whiskey - and her belly warms. She could bite him.

They pull apart and Jake holds out a chair for her. 'Here, here, sit.'

The room is back to spinning and Mary has to look down. It's so dark in the bar she feels like one more drink, it will swallow her up. She's hoping. And Jake's eyes sparkling like phosphorescence in the water. Mary sits.

Jake is still standing, now gripping the back of his chair. Dancing around it, Mary thinks, like he is going to launch into a cabaret number. It hits her he's nervous.

'You found it okay?'

'Yea, yea, no problem.'

She's wondering what he's thinking. What does he see? In his eyes she can read nothing - neither disappointment nor awe.

'Right, then I'll get us a drink. What are you having?'

Mary hates this question. And she hates her stock response, but she says it anyway - she figures, fuck it, she's out on the town. Jake can take her or leave her. At the end of the day, she'll be fine.

This is what she tells herself, before she says, 'I don't know. I'll have what you're having.'

And then she grins.

And he grins back.

And in that moment she knows everything is going to be all right.

'I was going to have a rum and Coke.'

'That sounds perfect!' She reaches for her wallet. 'Do you need money?'

But he just waves her away. 'Don't be silly. You can buy the next round.'

While he's up getting their drinks she has the luxury of watching him - and smoking a cigarette. From where she's sitting, she can stare openly at his backside as he leans into the bar. Now he is chatting with someone to his left, a short, slight man.

Mary takes a drag on her cigarette. Jake is taller than she imagined, and wiry and strong. Next to the man he's with at the bar he seems especially robust. His legs slightly bowed. With the red hair and the swagger, she keeps thinking of a cowboy. All he needs is a ten-gallon hat and a sprig of wheat sticking out his mouth.

Jake returns. The drinks fill a pint glass. Mary's looks practically black. Even with ice cubes it's the most sinister rum and Coke she's seen in her life. Remembers sherry and narcotics and smiles inside. Not Jake. And a gold chain visible around his neck. Did he buy it himself, or was it a gift? Something about it alternately repulses and excites her.

'So Mary.'

'Jake.'

She drinks again. Her enormous glass is already half empty. So is his.

'It's really nice to meet you, finally.' The way he says it, she can tell he likes her. 'So what do you think of Manchester?'

'Yea, it's great. I love it.'

'You're not disappointed?'

'Definitely not.' She's taking steady sips of her rum and Coke. It's strong but going down easily and fast. Her face burns, it must be as red as her dress. She's having a hard time meeting his eye. 'I'm really glad I came.'

'Yeah?'

'I don't get out much. Normally.'

'Man,' he says, looking away, shaking his head.

'What?'

'You know how cute you are, right?'

The room shakes and Mary's drink is gone. 'I'll go get us some more.'

To Mary's surprise the intense-looking man Jake was talking with at the bar is in her chair when she returns.

'Mary, this is my friend Paul.'

'Oh. Hi!'

'Mary, a pleasure-' Paul leaps from her seat, grabs a chair from another table and sits back down with them.

Up close his features are sharp. A diminutive Ralph Fiennes. Hairline receding to a point where there's only a faint tuft on the top of his head.

'Paul's an old friend. Mary, he's a theater director. A fellow Revolutionary,' Jake grins.

'Revolutionary?' Mary knows she should understand.

'The theater company? Have I told you about it?'

'Oh! Right,' Mary gushes, even though she's not sure. Takes a healthy swig of her drink. 'The Revolutionaries. The theater company.'

'This your first time in Manchester?' asks Paul. The question is conversational but his manner is blunt. Mary thinks of a hawk. In the darkness she can feel him checking her out.

'Yes,' she says, glancing at Jake, who smiles. 'It's really great,' she adds.

She knows it sounds stupid but it's the best she can do. Drunk and on the spot - he's Jake's friend, she wants him to like her.

'Jake says you're a playwright.'

'Um, yea. Well I-' she starts, but Paul cuts her off.

'Oh hey Jake, did you get a chance to check out that piece in *The Guardian* on Grandage?'

'I did.' Jake turns to her. 'Mary, do you see much theater in London?'

'Yea, um, not so much recently. But when I was on my course-'

'Paul just worked with Michael Grandage at the Donmar, did you see *The Cut*?'

'Oh, no. I didn't.'

'You did your degree in London?' Paul asks.

'Yup.'

Mary finishes her drink and smiles at Paul. He's pulling a pack of Silk Cuts from his pocket. She tries not to stare - now she wants one of her own Marlboros desperately - but she's not sure about smoking in front of Jake.

'So Mary,' says Paul. 'How do you two know each other?'

'Oh, ah...'

'She's friends with Roger Trumbull,' Jake says, as if that explains it.

'Ah.' Paul tips forward in his chair and lights up, exhales at the ceiling.

Jake continues, 'Mary wrote that dog monologue I was telling you about.'

'Gotcha,' says Paul. Then Mary catches him - when he thinks she's not looking, he winks.

Maybe Jake knows she's watching because he doesn't acknowledge it - doesn't even flinch. He's looking at Paul's cigarettes.

Then under the table she feels it - Jake presses his knee into hers. 'Hey Mary,' he says. 'You don't mind if I smoke?'

Her grin is enormous. 'I'm dying for a cigarette.'

They stay at Fab Cafe for at least two hours. Mary loses count of how many rounds. Drinking the pint-sized rum and Cokes.

To Mary's disappointment, Paul goes with them as they move on from bar to lounge to club. But the more she drinks, the less it matters. Sitting there as Jake and Paul talk over her head, she might be invisible. Means she can stare with abandon at Jake's eyes, the shape of his forehead. Imagines kissing him long before it actually happens. The way he touches her tips her off. He is hers. At least for the night. The way he asks her questions. The way he guides her along the blustery Manchester streets and alleyways.

When she finally grabs his face and kisses him they are standing at the edge of the dance floor in a gay club. Paul has long since vanished. Just the two of them kissing, they open their eyes to peek at the same time.

Sitting on a bench by the wall. Her legs draped over his lap. His hands on her face, on her back.

He stops and they stare eye-to-eye, foreheads pressed together.

'I never thought I'd get off with you.'

'You didn't?' Mary blinks. 'Why not?'

'I mean, it's not that I didn't want to - or hope that I might, it's just...'

'You said sherry and narcotics.'

'I did.' He is smiling now, then kissing her again. Kissing hard. Mary seeking to taste, beyond the alcohol and cigarettes. Inhales his lemony-cracker scent. Peeks again. His eyes are closed, pale lashes fluttering like he's having a dream.

Between her knees, a glimpse of his hands. Long and elegant. Covered with freckles.

She is straddling him with her red dress riding high when one of the bouncers taps her on the back. She and Jake startle.

'Take it home, eh?'

Jake grins and then hugs her close. They start kissing again.

'Ach - I mean it!'

Mary slides off and Jake makes a move to stand.

'Guess we better get the fuck out of here.'

'I'm ready,' says Mary.

Outside the club Mary leans against Jake. All around her, concrete and brick, flashes of light - from headlights, other clubs, all-night takeaways. She desperately wants to take a cab, but Jake already has his arm around her, urging her along.

'Where are we going?'

'The Britannia's this way- '

'You're taking me home?'

'It's late.'

'Yea - but…'

Mary is shocked, she's speechless. But she's afraid to protest or ask why. All she can manage is, 'Hang on.' Stops, tugs his coat-sleeve.

'What?' he asks. Then he sees. Takes her face in his hands and kisses the top of her nose. 'Fuck,' he says. Then kisses her for real, out there in the street, in the blistering cold.

Things blur, they are running. Jake holds her hand. Both of them breathing hard, coughing - all the cigarettes. Yet she is glad for the wind that presses them close.

'Goodnight Mary,' he says to her outside the Britannia.

'Goodnight Jake.' She doesn't dare press it. Tells herself he must be a gentleman - and isn't that what she wants?

He is all she wants, so she'll wait.

'Oh sweetheart,' Jake sighs.

'Jake.'

'Are you terribly disappointed?'

'Not at all.'

'Speak tomorrow, yeah?'

'Yes.' Mary looks up at him, smiles.

In the silence that follows, she suppresses more than a sigh. When he finally kisses her she's already thinking about the sherry she has left in her room.

She's up with the dawn. Watches the sky brightening, turning the curtains from grey to white. The rooftops and city skyline laced with gold.

Her belly is alive, the weight in her head lifts. Sits up for a cigarette, pours a tiny glass of sherry. Kicks back the sheets, then draws her knees up. Takes tiny sips, the warmth spreading inside her to match the rose-glow outside.

They do not meet again on this trip. He texts her that morning, at barely half seven.

> Sweetheart, miss you already. Wish I could have stayed with you last night - now stumbling about, semi-aroused…

The thought of Jake semi-aroused is almost too much. Mary takes a moment, lies face-up on the bed, and waits for the pounding inside her to slow down. Starts to touch herself and it helps.

Texts him back just before she steps in the shower.

> Thinking about you semi-aroused is a torment. Would that you were here with me right now. My train leaves at noon. Care to see me off?

He doesn't respond until nearly half nine. Mary is packed, ready to check out.

> Oh Mary, would love to see you off. With a kiss (several) sadly am tied up with errands. Will try to call in a bit. Xxx

Mary settles in a quiet corner of the Britannia lobby with her computer. Attempting to work, starts to wrestle with an essay by a Korean student applying to New York University. He writes of his dream of launching a fashion empire in the United States - 'utilizing cheap Korean labor.'

Mary sighs. Advises him to rephrase or cut the cheap labor bit. Suggests he emphasize instead his desire to use imported Korean textiles.

At quarter past eleven she still hasn't heard from Jake. Decides to head over to the train station. Walks slowly, in the brilliant sunshine. Taking in the shops, the route from the Britannia to Piccadilly now so familiar - Mary can't help entertaining the thought of moving there.

It wouldn't be so hard. Her job is portable, it might be nice to get away - get out of London. Hole up someplace she can write, focus on her play. Why not someplace nearer to Jake?

She's just boarded the train when he texts. Reads the message once she's settled by the window, her knapsack on the seat beside her.

> Mary! Are you on the train? God, I want to be with you. Care to text for a bit? Tell me what you are wearing...

Mary grins, sinks down low in her seat. The train has started to move. A businessman walks past, on his way from the food car with a can of Foster's and a sandwich. She waits until he passes, then writes,

> Jake, if you were here I'd be sat on your lap. In my tartan skirt, striped knee socks and fuzzy jumper...

7.

From: Mary Cartwright <mary_cartwright@editpro.com>
To: info@didsburyproperties
Subject: studio inquiry
Date: Fri, 20 Oct 2006 11:26 am

Hello,

I was just looking at your website- I am interested in renting a studio from 17/11/2006 for two months - or possibly longer - in Manchester/surrounding/Didsbury Park.

Your studios looked lovely and at 700/800pcm the price is right as well. I would love to know if you have anything available that might be suitable.

Thank you very much,
Kindest regards,
Mary Cartwright

***

'Could be the one you marry.'

'What?! But I'm not sure I'll ever get married-'

'Oh you will. It's in your chart.'

Mary's flatmate Gus is in his usual spot - sprawled on the couch in the dark with the TV on, dressed in his silk smoking jacket. By day he works at a travel agency in Knightsbridge, but his passion is astrology.

He takes a sip of wine, and eyes her like one of his subjects. 'He's a Gemini, isn't he?'

'Huh? Actually, I think he is, but-'

'Watch out. Probably has a big heart. Sharp, great talker. But Geminis have that Jekyl and Hyde thing going.'

'How'd you know his birth date?'

'I don't. But it's in your chart - a Gemini or Sagittarius is going to make a huge dent in your world. I'm making an educated guess. Don't spend any money on him, you'll be all right.'

'Um, okay.' Mary takes a seat on the floor by the couch. 'Wait. So I'm going to get married? And Jake could be the one?'

'Nothing definite. It's all up to you.'

'But you said it was in my chart.'

Gus sighs, takes a sip of wine. Eyes her like he is about to explain something to a very dense child. 'We all have certain transits in our charts, and these transits - the pull or influence of certain planets and combinations of planets - guide and influence us. They prompt us to make changes, certain choices. Still, it comes down to us. We don't need to act on these things.'

'O - kay.' Mary wants a cigarette, but she can only do that in the privacy of her own room, out the window.

'Secondary progressions reveal our cycles of maturity and growth.'

'Now you've lost me.'

'I can explain-'

'No its okay, Gus,' Mary smiles. She can tell by the dulled look in his eyes all he really wants is to get back to his wine and his Discovery Channel special on natural disasters. Gus loves shows on earth's catastrophes - tsunamis and earthquakes. 'If I wasn't an astrologer I'd probably be a tornado chaser,' he's said on numerous occasions. Somehow Mary finds it hard to imagine him out of his smoking jacket and dressed in storm-chasing gear - hollering at the back of a truck speeding towards an ominous cloud in the distance.

'Seriously, let me know. We'll sit down together and I'll go through your chart with you.'

'Cool.' Mary gets up off the floor. She knows it will never happen. Her housesit starts in a week, and when it's over, she's not planning to come back to Leicester Square. She's already given Gus her notice.

Back in her room, she opens her nightly bottle, the one she's picked up from the corner store at Shaftesbury and Dean. This time it's cider. Places it on the window ledge, alongside her cigarettes and green lighter.

She's still savoring her latest email from Jake.

> From: jakepverse@hotmail.com
> To: Mary Cartwright <scarymary666@yahoo.com>
> Subject: faith
> Date: Mon, 23 Oct 2006 8:27 pm
>
> Sweet Mary,
>
> You need to know this (I must say it again) you are about the only bright spot in my life these days. I know I have alluded before to certain complexities that have overshadowed this gingerman's existence as of late. Now you have come into my life I feel there is hope. (I promise to be more specific when next we meet. I'm picturing something along the lines of prostrating myself at your feet if I can manage to steal away & come visit you in London during your cushy sNotting hill pet-looking-after engagement.)But in the meantime Mary, I want you to know you are always at the forefront of my mind (and a welcome distraction) whilst I am mired the myriad messes that seem to comprise my life at present. (Mary, forgive me, it's been one of those days!) BTW, you know Annie Hall is one of my all-time favorite films? I've always wished I had a goofy American girl to hang out with- and now I do!

Mary sips her cider. Lights her cigarette while still inside the room, then quickly opens the sash and leans out the window. Watches the smoke trail across the rooftops, towards the fire station on the corner of Shaftesbury and Gerrard.

Already closing in on midnight and the revelers below have a fiercer pitch, a more violent tone. Maybe it's the cider or Gus's words, but Mary can't stop thinking of her father. What would he say about Jake?

He's gone but she keeps hearing what he says to her about men, about marriage.

'The thing is Mary, you're what, twenty-seven? You're in great shape, but you better get a move on, if you want to settle down.'

'Dad-'

It's the summer before he gets sick. They are out to dinner, just the two of them. Her heart is broken. She's just split with the one she thought was the love of her life.

'The thing is honey, guys your age don't know what they want...'

Her father has had two glasses of wine. She knows where this is going.

'What you need is an older man who will appreciate you.'

'Dad.' Mary is blushing, looking away. Willing her father's voice to go down. For him to stop talking altogether.

'Find an older guy, with some money.' Now he moves in close. 'The trick is to find some older guy and then fuck his brains out.'

'Dad-' Mary starts to leave her body, rises up so she's staring down at herself and her father at the table.

'Listen to me, fuck his brains out and then stop. Tell him you won't put out until he marries you.'

'Jesus Dad,' she says under her breath.

Her father leans back, pleased with himself. Polishes off the rest of his wine, his eyes with that sparkle.

***

From: Mary Cartwright <scarymary666@yahoo.com>
To: jakepverse@hotmail.com
Subject: mornin
Date: Wed, 25th Oct 2006 7:36 am

jake,

am in that huge starbucks on tottenham ct road under a too loud speaker, which means as soon as I finish my internet dealings I must bolt home to race through two edits I should have finished last night.

There is a businessman sitting a little too close across from me reading a book called "Healing the Modern Man's Soul."

am taking deep breaths so I dont panic about the crazy pile of edits on my plate. I wish I could just do my own stuff - get back to my play! I wish I wish I wish. I wish you were near...

From: jakepverse@hotmail.com
To: Mary Cartwright <scarymary@yahoo.com>
Subject: g'day
Date: Wed, 25th Oct 2006 9:13 am

Mary, I've had waaaay too much coffee. My head is spun (but mostly by you.) Do you have any idea how attractive you are? I think that you don't, which is enormously attractive. Everything about you - the way you dress, your intelligence- it almost feels like there's something larger than the two of us at play here. (I know it sounds new-agey and corny- and that's not me at all, I swear!) But I am so excited to see you again, to see where this goes! It's been so long since I've had a cool new person to hang out with. Hopefully I can come to sNotting Hill in one or two weeks time while you're looking after coddled kitty & cocker spaniel and we can play house!

jtpxxxxxxxxx

'Ah - allo, allo, come inside!' the Frenchman says when Mary arrives.

'Aymerick - hey, thanks.'

Mary sets down her knapsack and two extra bags. The sum total of her possessions.

'Jazzy, shush!' Aymerick scolds the rambunctious Cocker Spaniel at his heels.

Mary follows him down a long hallway. Ahead of them Jazzy tears madly up and down, slipping and sliding, claws scraping.

'Hey Jazzy,' Mary says, hoping to calm him, but it has no effect. The animal is purebred and mental.

Up the stairs, and into a lovely sitting room, with an open kitchen and dining room off to one side. An enormous window looks out on a private courtyard. Even though it's already the last day of October, the weather is mild, sunny. The window is open.

They sit at the table. Aymerick lights up a half-smoked, rolled cigarette.

'Yea, so I come back the 16th?' he says, exhaling.

The French and their cigarettes, thinks Mary. 'Cool,' she says.

'Alors,' he takes another drag and shoots up abruptly. His frame is lanky and thin. While his manner is scattered, his clothes are immaculate - a crisp teal Polo, cream-colored khaki's, perfectly pressed.

'I be off,' he continues, stubbing out his cigarette. 'You have my numbers - Vanessa too - I email you in the next day or so, ca va?'

'Sounds good.' Mary stands, trails behind him as he grabs his bags, a jacket, his keys.

'Jazzy, you be a gentleman.'

'Have a safe trip!' she calls after him.

Moments later, the front door slams and Mary is left standing in the hall. Jazzy stares up at her and she smiles back. 'Aren't we the lucky dogs?'

That first afternoon, she almost doesn't know what to do with herself. The day turns overcast and she can't bear to start work, so she decides to take Jazzy for a walk. They enter Hyde Park through the Orme Court gate. Cross the wide vistas, making their way parallel to the Bayswater Road. Stop to gaze at the statues, the Italian fountains. Then up by the ponds, along the equestrian track. Mary thinks of her father. How he hated horses - her passion as a little girl.

'People who ride horses are assholes,' he liked to say. Mary rode anyway, from the age of seven through her teens - until she discovered boys.

Now she watches a lone rider, a man on a splendid black gelding, cantering silently just beyond the trees. Hooves cupping and lifting off the soft dirt. He might be a mirage - something that exists in a world so beyond Mary's reach to be some kind of deity. A modern knight.

Mary realizes she's about to cry, the sadness welling up in her so profound and all-consuming she almost can't breathe. In the distance she can see the Lido - sturdy brown picnic tables, a concession stand.

'Come along Jazzy.' She wipes her eyes. Walks with renewed purpose. 'Let's see if they have any water.'

By the time they are making their way back up through Kensington Gardens it is dark out. Jazzy has gone docile, and she unclips his lead. Finds a few sticks, Mary hypnotized by the motion of throwing them as much as Jazzy is thrilled by it. No thoughts of anything else - not even Jake. People pass her like shadows.

When they decide to call it quits Jazzy is panting like an asthmatic.

'Hang in there boy, let's head home.'

Back in the flat, Mary feeds Jazzy and the plump kitty Gaspard. Ravenous herself, she drags a chair from the dining room into the kitchen and uses it to explore the depths of the cabinets. Finds a fancy-looking can of black beans, tiny ones, and heats them on the stove with some mustard.

Aymerick has a full bottle of Jameson's on the living room sideboard and Mary tells herself she's not going to touch it. Five minutes later she's tearing off the seal and pouring a small glass.

In the downstairs bathroom she finds the Valium and Percocet. Takes half a Percocet right then and there, already obsessing about when she will succumb to the Valium.

***

At work at the dining room table. Trying to. In her head, she's in full conversation with Jake. Telling him everything. All about Jazzy, the flat. Her one hand is typing, as fast as the auto-pilot side of her brain will allow.

> For this type of essay, the first paragraph is crucial - often it will determine whether admissions officers will continue reading the rest of your essay or not. A great technique is to craft an opening paragraph that is almost like a film clip - a live scene - that embodies what it is about bioinformatics that excites you...

Mary pauses to light a cigarette. Takes a careful sip of Jameson's. Pets Jazzy at her feet. He looks up at her with his exquisite black eyes. 'Good boy, Mr. Handsome,' she coos. Leans back in her chair, takes another drag and stares out at the garden.

From: Mary Cartwright <scarymary666@yahoo.com>
To: jakepverse@hotmail.com
Subject: hey hey hot spot!
Date: Tue, 31 Oct 2006 10:52 pm

just found the warm spot in the flat where I can get wireless! yoooheooo! right at the far end of the dining room table, near the MASSIVE window that looks out on the garden. this place is dope, dude.

I miss you.

but, I will be moving into didsbury park flt on nov 17th. hah!

there is a bottle of jamesons across from me, on the shelf. in the dining room here. yes, its that bigga house. has floors, upstairs, downstairs, bedrooms bathrooms. I get lost. I dont know what to do with all these rooms. I'm a one room gal.

okay. I want a teensy glass of the Jamesons. teeeeny. but that would be stooooopid. I have three more fucking essays to edit before the dawn.

I'm going to have a tiny sip.

please come visit me in grotty hill. come take a bath with me.

(oh god, I just noticed theres baileys too. I'm fucked.)

(just got up and had a bit of the baileys. yum. Im screwed. why do I do this to myself...)

She works through the night – there's a backlog of orders. Completes one every two hours. At four in the morning she gets up from her chair. Knows Jazzy should go out but she's afraid. London is dangerous like that. Even in the confines of the back garden, she's nervous, half expecting some baklava-ed intruder to hop over the high wall and molest her.

At six, when she does crawl into Aymerick's freshly made bed, the Valium she took on the home stretch of her last order is just kicking in. Spreading herself out the length of the bed sends synapses popping off all down her body like bubble wrap beneath a heavy roller.

Jazzy won't crawl beneath the covers with her, but she's happy with the way he plops down on her feet, pinning them to the mattress. The sun has almost come up completely, so the whole room is a warm shade of cream, glowing amber at the edges of the blinds where the pure light is seeping in.

Mary sets the alarm for nine and closes her eyes.

***

From: jakepverse@hotmail.com
To: Mary Cartwright <scarymary666@yahoo.com>
Subject: more drivel
Date: Wed, 1 Nov 2006 9:51 am

Mary, Mary, Mary...

I myself succumbed to one too many nips of the vodka last night so feeling summat under the weather. Thought I'd ride it out (at your expense) with an extended jaunt along the keyboard. Lucky, lucky you. I have to say, I'm quite envious of your continent-hopping editing-afforded lifestyle! Seriously. My world is infinitely less glamorous - compared to yours it's tedious, a bit weird and more often than not, rather thorny. Still having a hard time wrapping my head around the thought you are about to be my neighbor in Diddlesbury! Wild. Wonderful. But are you sure about this my dear? You really want to venture into the depths of Potterville? That said, you were all I could think about last night - just how excited I am to hang out with you. Lately I've been so weighted down by my dull troubles and disappointment. It's about time I had something (someone) to look forward to! Don't get me wrong- I'm not the high maintenance type- my baggage I keep securely locked away in my own deep storage. Oh, hey - by the way - thanks for your generous praise of my poem 'Fugue.' I always forget that one - it sort of wrote itself, actually penned it on my hand during a holiday in Portmeirion. In case you haven't noticed, I feel slightly underrated by the poetry community at-large. (More like, completely ignored!) I think I need to write a screenplay! Paul keeps suggesting it -

although I don't know the first thing about plots or narrative structure. Maybe that's why I'm a poet and an actor, not a playwright or a fiction writer, haha. I like to work backwards (backwords?) just fuss with shards I can't shake until they reveal themselves to me. Another thing you need to know is I'm broke. The last time I worked was last year, I did a few weeks on Hollyoaks. But my character was crushed by a lorry. Lately I've been thinking I may have to pick up a bartending gig - not an office job or anything full time- that would destroy me. Oh Mary, I must be honest. Things are precarious in my life right now. You've met me at an interesting time - or is that what everyone says? My plan was to get things sorted after the New Year - move house, strengthen my financial area - it's all kind of a mess right now. What's sprung up between us is a large part of what keeps me going these days! Maybe we could be like HG Wells and Rebecca West- one of those random, wonderful literary friendships! A few years ago I almost had something close, but in the end it was not meant to be. Clearly both of us are, shall we say, outside the mainstream in our approach to life - so together we ought to be...a force! Did you read that poem of mine 'Proviso' - it was in Ambit last year? Check it out if you can. It's particularly dear to my heart and I think you'll know what I mean. Anyway, no doubt you're reeling from the burnoff of my day-after vodka fumes. Keep fighting the good fight, sweetheart. Viva la revolution!

JTP xxxxxxxxxxxxxx

From: Mary Cartwright <scarymary666@yahoo.com>
To: jakepverse@hotmail.com
Subject: sunshine on my head
Date: Wed, 1 Nov 2006 11:57 am

Oh Jake, you INSPIRE me!

Jazzy and I just took our morning jaunt in the park- he was full o beans today so we walked long and far, until our feet were sore.

what. a. life. !!

god, jake, this flat is so beautiful, I feel like I'm on holiday. so quiet and full of charm and warm and cozy. where I sit and write at the dining room table by the window looking out over the garden, french doors and chandeliers and fireplaces- feels so grand and yet sweet and private all at once. I love it!

you've got me thinking so much about my PLAY.

feel like I need to now go back to my original vision, which was a narrative that is comprised of a series of beginnings- that all lead to the same center - with the first and last beginning being in fact two variations on the end (but one does not realize this until the play is over - because while they are watching it they are so utterly compelled but also trying to figure out (in a way that is not off-putting) what the hell is going on...)

okay, I dont expect any of this to make sense. am riffing.

at any rate, printing is going on as I write, and then there will be a splaying of acts and scenes throughout the dining room with judgment and killing of babies and preservation of others at hand...

do you have any idea yet when you might be able to come visit me? oh I hope you can come! darling I encourage you to be spontaneous and stagger onto a train any time between this moment and the 16th of Nov- whenever the mood should strike you.

darling sexy FUcK I wish you were here...

From: Mary Cartwright <scarymary666@yahoo.com>
To: jakepverse@hotmail.com
Subject: i will regret this
Date: Fri, 2 Nov 2006 1:15 am

can I send you a drunk email now?
just, I needto say...
argh. Jake. Im feeling dumb and ashamed bout my forwardness of late. I am not a sex addict. I am normally closed. I dont know. craP, but what was it? Oh. yea.

you need to know it's been some while (a year? no, more...) since I've even, well, been properly kissed. in other words, I haven't been with (touched) by a male-type perseon in a very long while. very. Long.

anyway, I need to end this before I do any FURTHER damage. lord knows I was headed that way despite all that I protest.ed.

mxxx

From: jakepverse@hotmail.com
To: Mary Cartwright <scarymary666@yahoo.com>
Subject: and do not hold this against me!
Date: Sat, 3 Nov 2006 10:42 pm

Sweets,

You remember that night you were here, what you kept saying to me? It was towards the end, so you might not- but no, I'm sure you do- you kept saying I was beautiful(!) Darling, I don't know what it is, but now girls everywhere I turn are smiling at me. It's uncanny! What have you done! It's had this strange effect- and to think what I might have been up to all these years if I had known. But sweetheart, don't fret, I'm saving every inch of my resplendence for you. I loved your drunk email by the way. Loved it because I could not have said it better (drunkenly) myself. It has been ages since I last hurled myself at a person of the female persuasion (and not ended up deflected into the gutter.) Don't be fooled by my performer exterior - I am no Casanova. If anything, I'm a bit of a recluse. Most days I barely set foot out my door. Honestly, it's just me in this big old house I share with a housemate who is never ever here. The arrangement might sound ideal, but in fact it's rather unusual for reasons I will explain to you the next time I see you (& once I have a great many drinks in me.) Just be forewarned. I've been planning to move house now for ages (almost as long as I've been so single!) I could probably use a swift kick in the arse - or rather, you know - somebody to galvanize me into action. What do you think? Do you have any desire to be my taskmaster? (I have to confess, just the thought of you as my master - task or otherwise - has me more than a little turned on!) Oh the monster you have unleashed! Are you really sure you want to get mixed up in the insane miasma that is Potterville? Not that I'm trying to dissuade you- I happen to be the greatest guy I know (!) But lately I haven't been feeling entirely myself - probably because things are so unsettled. Some days I feel I might burst. Or just- that I've somehow fallen through the cracks- or that the way my life has unfolded, I'm cornered. I do get scared I will end up like keats- except instead of penniless, alone and mortally ill, I'll be penniless, alone and drunk. And only decades after I'm long gone will my scribblings be recognized and lauded- by the very establishment that never even noticed me when I was here! Ah yes, a tale so unoriginal you must be dozing off- have I put you off me entirely? Blame it on that fourth cup of coffee- at this point I'm legally insane. Mary, I adore you, which unfortunately means I can't stop fretting you will be disappointed when you get here and truly grasp the boring truth of me! I'm pretty simple, flighty, fickle, a dreamer, a romantic - I like losing myself in characters onstage, and in my poems (because I myself am not so exciting.) And I do feel it, that our connection is such that at the very least we will be lifelong friends. We can walk through the parks, eat in dives and discuss poetry and plays. Except I have to be honest, at the moment I'm over poetry and theater. It's true, these days I'm into films - I think I mentioned I want to write a screenplay. Actually, it might sound weird, but this one poem I wrote has the seed for an amazing film - did you read 'Ponge Alone'? That would be Francis Ponge, of course. I was obsessed with him for a phase. I am a man of many heroes - Keats, Sam Shepard, Morrisey, Marlon Brando, Blanchot, Bob Dylan, Woody Allen to name just a few - don't worry, if you have not yet come to truly appreciate their greatness I will show you the way. Mary, darling, I am so sorry. I am so lost on a tangent I might never find my way back. Holy crap, I could be going prematurely senile - early onset alzheimers!

Seriously, delete this email!

Yours, most humbly.

jtpxxxxxxxxxxxxxxxx

***

'He's got to do something!' says Guinevere. 'How does he live?'

They are sitting in Victoria Park having an impromptu picnic. Mary has taken Jazzy on the Central Line from Notting Hill to Bethnal Green.

'Maybe he's got some money,' Mary says. 'Because seriously, it does seem like he stays home all day - maybe he has an inheritance? Not a lot, maybe it's just enough for him to be an actor slash poet and not have to work.'

'Perhaps. I don't see why you don't ask him.'

'I will,' says Mary, pulling out great hunks of grass with her fists.

'Don't do that sweetheart.'

'Sorry.'

Mary finishes the backwash left in her Carlsburg. Jazzy has stolen their empty hummus container. He holds it gripped between his paws, pulling at the plastic.

'I thought he was coming to Notting Hill? You guys were going to have a nice dirty weekend?'

'Yea,' says Mary. 'Me too, I was hoping. He just had too much going on.'

Guinevere sighs, takes the container from Jazzy, who looks at her hopefully, like she's going to throw it.

'You sure about this?' she asks.

'What, Manchester?'

'Yea.'

'I know it seems sudden. But seriously, it's not even about Jake, I'd want to go away somewhere anyway.'

Guinevere gives Mary a look so Mary knows she's not buying it.

'Okay,' says Mary. 'It's not just that he chose me, I feel like I'm ready to be attached. And I mean, how boring is life if we don't just go for it?'

Guinevere nods. 'I'm happy for you.' Looks Mary in the eye. 'Just know if anything happens, I'm here.'

***

From: Mary Cartwright <scarymary666@yahoo.com>
To: jakepverse@hotmail.com
Subject: Next week!
Date: Wed, 8 Nov 2006 8:25 pm

Jake!
I am so swamped with work and all I have wanted to do all day was respond to your email. I feel like my life is passing me by in this job. its fucked up. out of control. now I am grateful if I can go to bed like a regular person- that usually happens 2 nights out of seven, the rest I'm trying to keep my eyes ope banging

out these dumb essays on a deadline wondering what the fuck is going on. my little edit minions from china incessantly hounding me hounding me to transform their work so they might get into harvard business school and take over the world. while I stay in the same damn place, if less healthy, less rested, empty, spent... SPENT.

course, the alternative is loss of 'freedom' and possibly finding myself stranded living at my moms. I really have no other skills (that pay money) besides washing dishes! not to sound so dramatic. or baggagy. fuck I'm sorry.

Jake...I sense we are both odd birds in our way. I know I am. I too can entertain myself at the keyboard oblivious to the world for days, cracking myself up (that is, before the cyberedit egg fell on top of my head and smothered me!!)

its funny what you said about films. me TOOO. I've written a screenplay or two that I'm itching to pull back out and diddle with some more- jake, maybe we could write a screenplay together!(how many times you heard that one?!!) they are fun to collab on tho. theres a dumb short one I wrote on my myspace page. aaaannnyyywayy.

big kiss, dearest darling sexy superstar up north there.

weird. I will be there in a week, just about. a week from Thursday- tomorrow. dont worry. you'll hardly even notice. Im hard pressed to leave the house. maybe this will change.

I too fear one day winding up alone, penniless and drunk. splayed out at the wheel of my duct-taped together mac- the obvious thought is that maybe, at least, we can be peniless and drunk, but together. hoho.

mxxxx

From: jakepverse@hotmail.com
To: Mary Cartwright <scarymary666@yahoo.com>
Subject: Next week!
Date: Thur, 9 Nov 2006 9:52 am

Mary, Mary...

I've been up with the dawn, don't ask why - I haven't gotten anything more done. Gotten? Now you have me speaking American! Nothing much has changed over here. Haven't heard from any of the places I submitted my poems for weeks. No auditions for that matter either. Theater company in a deadlock on what show we're doing in the spring. Maybe you could write something for us? I'm only half kidding- with a fantastic meaty role for me! What do you think? We could pay you less than you earn in a day on your edits. No, but seriously, there's lots of young companies here and I will be sure to pimp your playwriterly ass when you arrive - it's a fantastic ass, too. And you will be here in a week! Although I'm not sure how I'm going to make it until then - the coming days promise nothing but torture and misery. (Why? My dear, I will save that for the promised conversation we will have when I see you- after we have had many, many drinks!) As for next weekend, my entire Saturday will be yours. Day and night. You can finally be bored nauseas by me in the flesh. Heck, I'll go the extra mile and lay gifts of my two poetry chapbooks at your feet! Because I am that kind of a guy. You know, even though I live just a few miles away, I hardly know diddleberry at all- it's where the posh folks live! So it might be fun to explore it with you. OR you could make the trek over here, to my fair village, Chorlton. In that case, the plan would involve a visit to my local where you could have the thrill of watching the football match with me, on a big screen TV, with endless pints and a roomful of working-class strangers. Sounds like a dream date, no? Oh Mary, please forgive me, I have to ask you one last thing. It's been on my mind, has done irreparable things to it in fact… the knee socks. Do you always wear them? I'm sorry I'm sorry - as I've said, I've been way too alone for way too long. I am overdue for a special new friend.
So...until soon - sparkle on my sweet!

From: Mary Cartwright <scarymary666@yahoo.com>
To: jakepverse@hotmail.com
Subject: Re: Next week!
Date: Thur, 9 Nov 2006 7:03 pm

baby, watching football in chorlton on saturday afternoon in a pub WITH YOU sounds tooo utterly divine to think about too much or I'll never get anything done. Oh yes, yes, yes. please lets. it would make my day. it would be awesome. yes.

jake, I am looking forward to having you as a new

friend too. we are from a similar planet. I too love being alone, can blissfully entertain myself and I think need the silence on some level too stay sane. I get jarred easily. but I do require a close friend or two to feel intensely loyal to and lay down and die for. or to believe in. maybe thats it. being alone is fine as long as I know I'm not 'alone alone.' the knowing someone is out there is everything- has a beauty in & of itself. you know. I blather..

anyway. in answer to your question, yes, I do tend to wear knee socks all the time, striped but sometimes cabled or otherwise patterned. and the beauty of spending most of my time alone is not having to dress appropriately for public which means I usually spend my time in various stages of undress, because, well, I do enjoy my body, but it took a long time. I feel like my life changed, just blew wide open- in a good, let the sunshine in kinda way- the moment I learned to love my ass. the rest of the body followed.

blah blah blah.
jake. right now i am wearing a little velvet skirt I just had taken in cause it was too big in the waist and kept falling off, my red & black striped knee socks and a very small very white baby t (braless, but of course- when the shirt is tight...)my hair is sooooo long these days, now it is halfway down my back, such a weird feeling for it to be so long. I put red lipstick on earlier to test it out and now its at a perfect fade. very bruisy-red. I like it.

Jazzy is noisily chewing a huge bone I bought in an effort to get him off my back- he is such a spoiled pest- darkness falls on notting hill and I have 3 hours to edit a 4page essay by a Korean girl who want to dedicate her life to social work...

but. I am sparkling. because I know you are out there...

9.

'Stop - here is good. You can just pull over here...'

The driver raises an eyebrow through the rearview mirror. 'You sure?'

'Yea. Should be one of the ones along here.'

'You want me to pull in up there?'

'Uh, yea. Cool.' Mary isn't sure it's the right house, but something in her gut tells her they're close.

Now she's in Didsbury everything looks imposing and overgrown, the numbers of the houses obscured by great hedges and stone walls.

The minivan shoots up what turns out to be a circular drive and then slams to a halt in front of a large, somewhat dilapidated manor house - Georgian or Victorian - made of enormous rust-colored stone blocks.

Mary hesitates before getting out.

'You want me to wait?' the driver asks.

'Um, I should be okay.' She's had a hand on her wallet the whole ride. 'What do I owe you?'

'Ah, eight quid.'

Mary gives the driver a ten-pound note. 'Keep the change.'

'You sure you don't want me to wait?'

'No, really. I'm cool. Thanks again.' She waves him off. Tires in reverse screech on the gravel.

When he's gone, Mary stands, taking in the silence. Save for the birds and the hum of the motorway in the distance all is still. Not a single car goes past on the street, there's nobody on the sidewalk. Despite the fact it's already mid-November, she's taken by the lushness of the place. After so much time in central London, the secluded enclave has a Southern Gothic feel.

She picks up her bags, and heads for the front door. Now she can see the number, she's sure it's the right place. The building is enormous. She can tell it goes on for ages inside. But it's also what her parents might have called a 'handyman's special.'

The front door is open and she steps onto the landing, then tries the inner door, which is unlocked as well.

'Hello?'

The foyer is dusty and littered with mail and random flyers. There is a grand staircase leading up to the second floor, and a small ladder and opened toolbox off to one side. Down a short hallway are doors to what Mary assumes are the flats. The one nearest to where she is standing opens and a man steps out - so tall and thin Mary thinks of a Praying Mantis.

'Hello - Ira?'

'Mary? You made it.' He holds out his hand, smiles beneath a sandy brown moustache. His hair hangs in a ponytail that goes all the way down his back.

'Yea, hi,' says Mary.

'Well, come, come. Right this way. The cleaners are just finishing up, but if you don't mind waiting. Should only be another ten minutes or so.'

The flat is beyond anything she could have hoped for - cathedral ceilings, enormous windows, hardwood floors - even a chandelier. Aside from the housesit, it's the most beautiful place she's ever had all to herself.

'The bed comes down like this-' Ira is saying, over by the far wall. Undoes a latch so what looks like a cupboard is released, revealing a queen-sized bed. The studio is so large it seems silly the bed would ever need to be folded away.

'And the couch comes out as well, in case you'd rather sleep there-'

Mary wanders towards the bathroom, near the entrance to the flat. Peering in she sees one of the cleaners perched at the edge of a clover-shaped tub.

'I'll be finished here in a minute,' the woman says with a smile. Her hair is pulled back in a bandanna and Mary is embarrassed that that an actual team of cleaners is at work on what is to be her flat.

'No problem, thanks.' Mary smiles back at the woman, who doesn't look up. The faucet is on and she's scrubbing with vigor.

Back in the main room Ira is checking light bulbs and opening drawers. The studio has an open plan kitchen, complete with a little bar. Perched on a stool there, Mary can look directly out the large front windows.

'Oh my gosh. This is amazing,' she says again. Feels like she's said it a million times.

Her hand is back on her wallet. With no UK bank account, she has to pay cash. It's taken her three days, making withdrawals from an ATM machine. Now she has just over seven hundred pounds. She's hoping it's enough.

Ira is still poking about and their lack of conversation is becoming nerve-wracking. The cleaners are still at work. The woman in the bathroom now has the shower on, while another woman is doing a final wipe-down of the kitchen.

Outside the sun is setting rapidly. The fading of the light in its chilliness has a stony beauty and Mary is gripped with anxiety - not related to her edits this time. She is alone, in a foreign country. In a random village, someplace she's never been before, where she knows no one. Her nearest friends are several hours away.

'Oh - and here's the phone-' Ira pulls an old brown handset with an overstretched and tangled cord from out one of the desk drawers. 'Ah, let's see here...'

He appears to be looking for an outlet, and Mary stands up to help him. 'There,' she says, pointing to a socket over by the fridge.

'Ah yes.' He plugs it in and lifts the receiver. 'Seems to be working all right.'

'Great.' An awkward silence. 'This is just amazing.' Mary says it before she can stop herself. But she manages to catch Ira's eye as she does so. Makes a move with the hand in her pocket and boldly brings out her overstuffed wallet.

She's counted the bills carefully in private, already grouped them in sets of hundreds, each one wrapped in an elastic hair band.

'Cash okay?'

'Cash is great.'

'Ah...so what is it again?'

'Seven hundred,' says Ira primly.

'Right,' says Mary. In the context of her life up to this point, the amount is astronomical. But editing around the clock, she's earned it. Only she won't be able to stay more than two or three months. Come spring, when applications to college and graduate school subside, so will her income.

Mary sets out her seven stacks of twenty-pound notes, hoping Ira hasn't noticed how her hands are shaking.

Ira counts the money again, right in front of her. It seems to take ages. 'Right then,' he says when he's finished. 'I guess I'll be off.'

'Thank you so much,' she says. Notices the cleaners have left.

'Call me if you need anything, there's a list of numbers on the fridge.'

'Yes, thanks.' She just wants him to be gone.

Once she's standing alone in the studio it seems even bigger. It has a dorm-like quality and Mary decides it's the décor. The furniture is cheap and generic, yet the overall effect is cheerful. The bedding will have to be overhauled - a worn blue duvet cover that looks like it belongs in a teenaged boy's room. The pillows are flat and limp.

Mary places her bags on the bed and manages to get two opened and half of one unpacked. Finds some PG Tips in a jar on the kitchen counter, fills the electric kettle and makes herself a cup of black tea. Explores the drawers and cabinets, filled with mismatched dishes, silverware, and a few worn pots and saucepans.

Drifts into the bathroom. Starts to run a bath, then turns on the shower. Sticks her hand in, testing the water. The pressure is strong, not the dribble she's become accustomed to in London - even Notting Hill. Before she takes off her clothes, she changes her mind. Turns off the shower and looks at herself in the mirror - it's already steamed up. Her eyes have deep circles. She hardly slept at all the night before - the edits, she was so excited. Promises herself, now she's made it to Didsbury, she'll go to bed early.

It's not yet five o'clock. Nearly dark. Mary decides to leave everything where it is and head out for a walk. Grabs her coat, closes the blinds. Conscious of not having a dog at her heels - it feels strange.

Stepping out on the front stoop she is again moved by the silence. The neighborhood is still. Not a human in sight. She curses herself for not asking Ira more about the village of Didsbury. For starters, where it is.

At the end of the street, she comes upon Didsbury Park. The sun is now completely disappeared from the horizon. Wishes her jacket was warmer. Crossing the park, her thoughts return to Jake. What is he doing at this very moment? Checks her phone. It's just gone past five - she texted him at half two, when her train arrived at Piccadilly Station.

That's nothing, she tells herself. Not even three hours.

Emerging from the park through a different exit, she's relieved to find herself at the far end of what is definitely a main road. Now there's cars whizzing past, people about - and best of all, Christmas lights, already up! Her comfort-level rises as she passes a chain restaurant she knows from London - Pizza Express.

At an intersection she spots three wine shops, one on each corner. Her own Bermuda Triangle. Now her phone vibrates in her pocket. It has to be Jake.

> You're here! Fantastic! See you tomorrow - will text you mid-day so we can make a plan. XojtpoX

Mary beams. More than contagious, her joy is like a magnet. People passing don't just smile, they nod and say 'Hi' or 'Good evening.'

She crosses the street and stops first in a cheese shop. It's crowded and warm, everyone pushed up against the counter - a vast display of exotic cheeses. Mary is glad for the mob. It gives her more time to decide. When at last it's her turn, she's still not sure.

The clerk prompts her, 'This cranberry Brie? A Roquefort? A baguette? Our very own caramelized onion spread, made right in the store?'

Mary says yes to everything he suggests, one hand tight on her cash. When she pays she makes certain she still has several large notes left for the wine.

For that she chooses the shop on the far corner, closest to home. A large, cavernous place, tastefully done up like most yuppie wine boutiques. Though well past the legal drinking age, every time she enters a liquor store she feels like a child, like she shouldn't be in there. When asked for ID, she's always more nervous than flattered.

The selection is vast. She does her best to look like she knows what she wants - something other than Jacobs Creek or Concha y Torro. She's poking around the Chilean reds when a young man approaches her.

'Can I help you find anything?'

He's large, well over six feet and built like a bear, dressed in boxy jeans and a black shirt. His hair is shocking, a dirty blonde white-man's 'fro.

'Um, how's this?' Mary pulls a bottle at random off the rack.

'Yeah, that's okay, but I tell you what, we're having a special on the Australian Shiraz. Two bottles, get the third one free.'

'Sounds perfect,' she says even though she's never been keen on Shiraz. Not until the guy is ringing her up does she notice each bottle costs twenty-two quid. Even with the freebie thrown in, it hurts. She will have to be far more careful with her money. Her next paycheck is more than a week away, and she now has less than fifty pounds cash to her name.

The clerk takes his time wrapping each bottle in tissue before placing it in a fancy shopping bag. They never did that with the cheap bottles she used to buy at the mini-mart on Shaftesbury Ave.

Back on the sidewalk, the village is beginning to empty and the temperature has dropped. With one hand gripping her collar closed around her neck, and the other hugging her shopping bags to her chest, she breaks into a jog.

The flat is so warm, so cozy when she returns. With all the lights on, beyond the large windows it's pitch black, and she debates whether to leave the shades drawn or up - anybody passing by would see her illuminated, see every last detail of the studio's interior. The moon is a sliver, bright yellow, high above the trees and she likes having it in view. The shades go up.

What to do first? Leaves the bags on the counter, and locates a corkscrew. Opens a bottle and pours herself a glass. Takes her first sip of wine. She's in Manchester, finally. For the foreseeable future - in her very own studio flat.

A little more wine and something softens, the longing slips in. A strong urge to call her mother. She's so far away. Mary lights a cigarette, tells herself she'll call tomorrow - or send an email. Her mother knows about Jake, but only that they are 'dating.' Has no idea Mary is no longer in London.

But once Mary's started drinking, any form of communication with her mother is dangerous.

Instead, she goes to the window near the bed and opens it. Crawls out and sits on the ledge. A stiff wind rattles the trees, their leaves reflecting the light from the nearest street lamp. Mary takes a long drag, excitement building in her chest - like she could inhale the whole world and still have adrenaline to spare.

10.

From: Mary Cartwright <scarymary666@yahoo.com>
To: jakepverse@hotmail.com
Subject: heaven
Date: Sat, 18 Nov 2006 9:47 am

baby,
I am in such bliss, although shopping is in order, which I hate.
but,
can I just say?
HUGE windows looking out on sleepy leafy quiet street
high ceilings...
big desk (faced out huge windows...)
pink clover-shaped tub (bet you didnt see that one coming- me neither.) but its great-
has a SHELF!!! (crazy and absurd but totally endearing, just how I like it.)
the kitchen rocks.
the garden is a fairy land....
if I only had a dog.
oh.
well.
at least I have you.
(see you in a few hours!)

By noon Mary is primed for his text. Maybe he'll even call. Doesn't dwell on the fact they've never once talked on the phone. Dressed in her tartan and fuzzy jumper, knee socks and pea coat, she's ready to go. Will they meet at the pub? She expects so - has already looked up the car service number for the quick trip to Chorlton. According to the Manchester A to Z it's just up the road. So close she could probably walk, but outside it's cold, her make-up is perfect, her hair curled just so.

Half twelve, she goes online - no emails, her edits are finished, she's taken herself off the rotation until Sunday evening. Plenty of time, she hopes, to spend a lazy morning-after with Jake.

At one fifteen, she pours herself a glass of wine - just a small one. The game starts at three, so really there's plenty of time. Mid-day could be closer to two or two-thirty.

By one forty-five it's clear she won't last knocking about in her studio. Maybe she will walk - if she starts towards Chorlton, does some exploring, she should arrive just in time for the game. When he does text her, she'll already be nearly there. Yes. That's what she'll do.

Only thing is, her outfit. Bare knees in the middle of November - she's going to freeze. But she can't bear to put pants on, so she allows herself another glass of wine.

In the village, in broad daylight, Mary is just as enchanted as she was the night before. Now instead of the cheese shop and wine stores, she explores the charity shops and specialty stores. At an upscale kitchen and cookware boutique she finds woks on sale, and resolves to buy one. The idea of cooking for Jake opens up new vistas of delight.

Wanders over to the library, ventures inside. The collection is small, but the building is charming. Flyers in the entranceway advertising poetry readings - she scans them for Jake. The she sees it - a yellow flyer - she recognizes the name: The Revolutionaries. An announcement for a staged reading, the play is 'Shopping & Fucking' by Mark Ravenhill. Jake is listed among the cast. Directed by Paul Baggot, surely the same Paul from the night she and Jake first met. The date, she notices with some disappointment, is long past. The first of September.

Mary checks to see if anyone is looking, then takes the flyer down, folds it carefully, and slips it in her pocket.

Half two, still no word from Jake. She's not sure if she should text him - but he's said he will get in touch with her. Patience.

Checks her A to Z. If she follows the Barlow Moor Road to the left, she should wind up in Chorlton.

At first she's cold, self-conscious in her knee socks and short skirt. A lone girl, walking along the road. Nobody on the sidewalk in either direction. The cars are sporadic. The sun has disappeared leaving behind a heavy grey sky. It's just gone 3:00. The game must be starting.

Standing at the curb on the brink of a massive intersection, Mary's fear is like a thin blade at her belly. Up ahead, on the other side of the six-lane road is a cemetery. With no walk signal, she must wait for a break in the oncoming traffic. The cars race by at ferocious speeds. Now it's so cold she might be standing there naked.

Still, she waits and watches. And then a brief lull - a matter of seconds. Mary holds her kilt down with both hands and makes a run for it, reaches the other side, panting. To her right, the gravestones in the cemetery seem to be mocking her. The ones knocked down, slayed by the hilarity of her predicament. Fear continues to flutter in her chest. But she thinks of Jake, wraps her jacket round tighter, ducks her head to the wind. Walks briskly - might be race-walking. The cemetery to one side, stones black with mold, guarded by hunched-over trees and draped in tangled vines. Ahead is a crematorium, but before she reaches it, she crosses the road. Now she's on the side lined with shabby brick houses, several tombstone stores, shoddy mini-marts.

Notices the gang of kids when it's too late to cross back. Maybe seven or eight of them, several on bikes, dressed in baggy pants, hoodies - a few in baseball caps.

Mary curses herself. In her tartan skirt and knee socks she's hard to miss. Feels them staring. Keeps her head down. Tells herself with kids, like dogs, it's best to carry on as if nothing is amiss. Fear smells. Hopes her own is not too obvious.

With less than ten yards to go before she must pass them, she senses they have stopped what they were doing, are waiting for her. She doesn't dare look up. To calm herself, she imagines she's anywhere else - South Beach, Miami comes to mind. Pictures herself in the hot sun, strolling along the boardwalk, surrounded by tanned friendly Americans in bathing suits and shades.

'Oi!'

'Slag.'

Still Mary does not look up.

'Oi! You there!

'Ha! Fekkin bird's movin. Racaaaa,' says another.

Mary hears a 'whack' and realizes several of them have hockey sticks. Head down, eyes closed, she's just about to pass. The only sound the clack-clack of her pumps on the concrete.

But walk by them she does, and nothing happens. They might have reached out and grabbed her - or worse - but they don't. Her relief is profound.

She moves at such a clip that soon there's enough space between them again, she can look up. She's sweating in spite of the cold. Dizzy, short of breath - but oh, the relief. After another fifty or so yards, she looks back. The kids are still there, but no longer looking at her. She pauses. Lights a cigarette.

The stores are slightly more inviting. Across the street, a park and an elementary school. The road slopes downhill until just before a Blockbuster, when it curves back up again. Several yards beyond that, she sees a bus station, a Cooperative market, and a ratty-looking charity shop with bins of bric-a-brac and books outside.

Quarter to four. Surely the game is still on. Now she's in Chorlton, the whole expedition feels like a horrible mistake. Her outfit is ridiculous, she's frozen, exhausted - doesn't even want to think about what's become of her makeup, her face.

At the bus station she considers hopping on board. The bus back to Didsbury idles at the stop. Goes as far as buying a ticket, but something inside her is not ready to give up. It could still happen - her dream afternoon with Jake - watching football in the pub, drinking pints with his friends.

Something must have delayed him - maybe he's on his way right now, about to text her.

She continues up the road, goes left, and spots an Oxfam bookshop just beyond a Woolworths. A perfect place to kill time. If she hears nothing by half four, she'll text him herself. Nothing wrong with that - they had plans.

The guy at the counter is skinny and pale. Reading George Orwell's *Nineteen Eighty-Four*. Mary's convinced that inside he's mocking her costume. She heads to the Drama section, scanning for Behn or Kane. Spots a tempting Pinter collection, but it's too thick to carry around.

Five minutes to four, but Mary's trying not look. And then it happens. Her phone vibrates.

> Mary, so sorry - something came up & just at the pub now. let's meet at yours @ 7ish? txt me your address. xoj

***

Mary takes the bus. She sits towards the front, avoiding the stares of two old ladies seated across from her. Looking at her like she's a tart.

Well I guess I am. Presses her forehead to the window, looking out. The bus passes the stretch where the kids had been, but now they are gone. Just a lonely stretch of sidewalk, littered with empty crisp packets and soda cans.

Back in her studio, Mary takes a bottle of wine down from on top of the fridge. Pours a large glass and drinks without holding back. Twenty minutes later she's nearly finished the bottle. No big deal. She showers, downs the rest standing at the kitchen counter, dripping wet, wrapped in a towel. Goes ahead and opens another bottle - why not? Jake's on his way over. At last.

She gets dressed, chain-smoking cigarettes so she has to open a window. Plays music off her computer, dances around. When she's nearly finished the second bottle Jake texts.

on my wat, hav had quite abit 2 drink at pub.xxxx

She's twirling in her tartan, pulling her jumper up, wiping the sweat from her chest. Head spinning. Feeling gorgeous. Face in the mirror - more lipstick, more eyeliner, more blush. Takes out the cheese, then forgets it. Knocks the baguette to the floor. Never picks it up.

Small bits of gravel banging on the window. When did she close it? At first she carries on like it has nothing to do with her. Then she realizes: someone is outside. Jake has arrived and the buzzer is broken. Barefoot, she stumbles out the flat to let him in.

11.

The first time she wakes, it's dark out. Dawn. Jake still has his arms around her. In sleep, his face is calm - he looks so young. Eyelids trembling. Thinks she sees the faintest hint of a smile.

Knows right away it's Sunday. Knows where she is. Knows she doesn't need to tend to edits.

Can't remember anything - the night before. Stares again at Jake. His gentle breathing. Rust stubble on his cheek.

Slides a leg along his body under the covers. Skin on skin. They had to get to this place somehow. The last thing she remembers, pebbles at the window. Nothing else.

Later still. Daylight on a white canvas - the drawn shades. Wavering ever so slightly in the faintest draft, shadows of leaves dancing behind them.

'Hey.' Jake kisses her cheek.

'Hey.' Mary looks up. Kisses his chin. Bursts of energy - need, thrill and happiness - ripple through her.

'What time is it?' Underneath the covers, his hand grazes her waist.

She shudders. Finds her phone. 'A little after nine.' Goes to put it down on the chair next to the bed and drops it. 'Whoops.'

They both giggle. Kiss.

'Morning.'

'Morning sunshine.'

Cool fingertips on warm skin, everything so soft. Smells like bodies, lemon, sweets.

'I'll be right back,' she whispers, slipping from the bed. Naked, sprints to the bathroom. Conscious of her ass.

When she returns Jake has rolled over, he's grinning.

'Thought you'd ditched me.'

'Never.'

She runs the last few feet to the bed, leaps in and wiggles up next to him. Peeks beneath the sheets, his body a mass of freckles on pale, pale skin. Tufts of auburn in places that excite her. He's kissing her neck, her cheeks, her eyelids, her lips. She's glad she brushed her teeth - but likes that he hasn't.

She might be touching him for the first time. Admires the creamy arc of his shoulder. Closes her eyes and slides a hand down along his arm to his hip. He does the same.

'Come here you,' he says, but she's already climbed on top.

Straddling him, leaning in close, eyes closed, wet hot, her nipples graze his skin. He leans up and kisses her, hard.

Cradled cheek to chest, the length of her body spread upon him. Rubs her feet against his.

'Happy feet,' she says.

'What's that?'

'My foot wiggle. What my dad used to call it.'

'I do that too - helps me get to sleep.'

'Me too.'

Looking into each other's eyes. Barely blinking, slowly breaking into a smile. Fingers intertwined.

***

'Want some coffee?' she says, slipping out the bed. The room is cold.

'I'd love some!'

'No more instant for you-'

'You're an angel-'

'I have French press.'

Mary reaches for a sweatshirt on the chair. Spots her clothes from the night before in a pile by the couch. Has no memory of taking them off.

Before she's out of reach he's grabbed her, pulls her back to bed.

'Ja-ke!' she's giggling, rolling over on top of him. He's blowing gently on her face, sticks his tongue in her ear.

'Oh my God!' She squirms away, now he's tickling her. 'Aaah, stop-'

'I got you-'

'I'm - so - tickle - ish. No!'

He stops. The two of them on their backs, winded.

'I can't believe you're here,' she says.

'Neither can I.'

Another silence, only the sound of their breath.

'So how about that coffee?'

'Jake!' She swats him with a pillow.

'Kidding - not!'

'I'll make you breakfast.' She sits up again, searches the floor for more to wear.

'I won't stop you,' he says. Rests his chin on her shoulder, holds her from behind. Thumbs her nipple and she goes still, lets the sensations rip through her.

'This is excellent,' he says.

She makes his coffee sweet and strong, heats the milk on the stove.

'Good,' she smiles.

The way he's sitting in her bed, bare-chested, sheets to his waist, she wants to frame him. His copper hair all scruffy, translucent in the sunlight.

'Hey,' he says.

'What?'

Now she's perched on her knees at his side. He leans over, his kiss tastes like Coffee Nibs. His tongue sends fresh shivers through her, she's wet again.

She prepares a feast. A heavy-handed American version of the full English breakfast. Makes it her own way, with toast, scrambled eggs, sausages and bacon, baked beans and grilled tomatoes. Extra spicy mustard, ketchup and Tabasco.

'You like the hot sauce,' he says, as she douses her eggs.

'Check it out.'

Jake's eyes go wide. 'You're going to burn a hole.'

'Nah.' Mary scoops a large pile of beans on her fork all smeared in egg yolk.

'Still,' he says. 'It's excessive.'

'You think?' she asks, her mouth full.

'I do.' He sets down his plate.

She puts down her plate too. Swallows, wipes the thin layer of Tabasco-induced sweat from her brow. Crawls over to him and curls up next to his belly.

In the silence, shadow fairies flit in patches of light along the walls. Mary plays with the fuzzy hair on his arms.

***

'I need to go.'

'No!' She sits up, 'I mean, do you? Really?'

The room smells of the feast they've only half devoured. Now congealing on their plates by the bed.

Mary's desperate for him to stay. The sun is shining - she can think of countless plans for the afternoon. None involve his leaving. Everything depends on his being there with her. Spending the day in bed. Exploring Didsbury. A long walk. Talking for hours.

'Could you pass me my pants?'

'Huh?'

'I think they're over there in the corner, I just want to check my phone.'

'Oh, of course!' She leaps off the bed, finds his crumpled navy cords - the thick kind. 'Here.'

'Thanks.'

Mary turns her back to him and hums, picks up their dirty dishes, their mugs. Brings everything to the sink. On the counter she sees the plate of bread and cheese she prepared the night before. Untouched.

'Hey cupcake. Sorry about that.' He puts his phone away. 'Shall we go for a walk?'

Her spirits soar. All is well and as it should be. Better than that - he's not leaving yet. Her doubts, reservations, suspicions dashed. Everything is still perfect.

'I'd love to,' she says. 'Let's get dressed.'

Leaving the flat, he insists on bringing his 'man bag.'

'You don't mind?' he asks.

'What? Uh, no. Course not.' But as she says it she's not sure what she's supposed to mind - that he's bringing the bag with them on their walk? That he's going to be leaving.

He's using the walk as a circuitous way out.

He waits patiently in the hall as she locks her front door. She's dressed sensibly this time - no more knee socks, bare legs and skimpy jumpers. Has on her navy blue chinos, thick socks, Converse. She's dressed to walk for hours.

They exit her building and pause in the driveway. She pulls out her cigarettes and he grins.

'Was afraid to ask.' He takes one from her.

'I know,' she says. 'I just put my hands in my pocket and there they were.'

She lights them both. 'It's a good omen,' she says, meaning the match didn't go out.

'You're funny,' he says, and her heart swells. 'So, which way should we head?'

'Well,' she says, taking a drag and pointing off to the right, towards the park. 'I've been over there, explored the village.' She takes another drag, blows smoke, looks the other way. 'But I kind of want to see what's in that direction. Supposed to be a massive Tesco's not too far.'

'Sounds good to me.'

So off they head. Jake seems awkward with his bag.

'What's in there?' she asks. 'Looks heavy.'

'Mostly books, plays.' He's leading her down a side street. Large family houses, all red brick and white aluminum siding, driveways with two cars.

'You brought that to the pub?'

'Yeah. But I hide it the moment I get there. So far no one's really noticed I don't think.'

'You'd get beat up?'

He laughs, 'Oh no. They're not like that.'

'Your friends?'

'Yeah, well.' He doesn't elaborate, and she doesn't press for more.

Not ten minutes later, they're lost. Reached a dead end.

'I feel like if we could just cut through,' Mary points towards the garden of a particularly large house.

'Definitely sounds like the motorway over there.'

Mary nods, 'And probably the Tesco's.'

Jake is looking at his watch, fidgeting. Mary knows he wants to leave and now she's okay with it. As much as she's anxious about his departure, it's inevitable, and on some level will be a relief. To be alone again, so she can savor everything.

They backtrack the way they came. Out the cul-de-sac, onto the park lane, forty yards or so to Mary's building.

'I'll call you a car.'

'I can take the bus.' He says it like 'boos' with his Northern accent. She loves it, stores the phrase in the sound of his voice for later.

'Baby, take a car - I insist - I'll pay for it.' As she says it, she knows it's outrageous. Yet she can't bear the thought of him on the bus, alone. In public, without her.

'Don't be silly.' He's kissing her nose. 'I've got it.'

Mary runs inside to find the card with the car service number. Jake waits on the stoop with a cigarette. When she joins him he gives it to her.

'You take the rest.'

'You sure?'

'Yea,' he says. 'I don't like to smoke at home.'

The car comes so fast they might be the only people in the entire village. Jake goes to kiss her on the cheek, but she's having none of it. Kisses him on the lips, holds him there. And he succumbs, takes her back.

'Sweetpea,' he says at last, pulling away. 'I really need to go.' Squeezes her arm, then ducks inside the car. Mary does her best to be stoic, still she can't help feeling betrayed. Breaks down, slips him a twenty-pound note through the window.

'Darling, no,' he says as he takes it.

'Thank you,' she says.

'Thank *you*,' he says. The driver is waiting. 'Talk later,' he waves. 'Stay sweet.'

The car pulls away. She watches it, until it has turned the corner, picking up speed past the park. Disappearing from sight.

Back in the flat, she's not ready to clean up. Something inside her is threatening to plummet. By evening she will have to face her emails, new orders will be trickling in. A backlog of client questions to face.

She stands in her studio, still holding her keys. Does not take off her jacket. Instead she waits a few moments. Then puts her hands in her pockets, turns, and heads back outside.

She walks a lap around the park - empty save for a middle-aged man on a jog. His shorts are white and he's in a blue jersey, passes her twice. Mary thinks about exercise, imagines going for a run every morning. She's still in shape. All her long walks with Jazzy, swimming in the outdoor pool at Covent Garden. Already it feels like ages ago.

At Marks and Spencer she buys dish liquid, lemon squash and chocolate. Goes home and cleans the flat until it's spotless. Does it with the TV on for company - all the lights on too.

Still not ready to work.

She heads back out. Goes opposite the park, the way she went with Jake. Walks with purpose, a little scared now it's dark. If a gang of kids materialized she'd be defenseless.

Plunging onwards. Another intersection, one that hints of activity and civilization. Waiting for the light to change, she spots a drycleaners, a computer store, a tax preparer's office.

The drycleaner's is open, a blonde woman at the counter poring over a crossword puzzle. Mary enters and the woman looks up. Her smile is nicer than Mary could have hoped for.

'Hi,' says Mary.

'Hello. You picking up?'

'Oh, um. No - no.' Catches the woman's eye, takes in her raspberry top. Reminds Mary of a jumper her own mother has. 'You do drop-off?' she asks.

'Yes, yes we do,' says the woman.

'Cool. Great, that's great.' Mary's face is hot. 'I just moved...'

The woman looks at her with vacant eyes, but still smiling.

'Tesco's is that way?' Mary asks.

'Ah, yes it is. Just keep going straight past the roundabout, can't miss it.'

'Thank you,' Mary nods, catches herself mid-bow. 'Thanks!'

Back out on the sidewalk she's relieved and uplifted. Sees the Tesco's just as the woman promised. Excitement. Adventure. A foreign superstore. Like wandering into a travel agency to window shop all the places she might go if she had the money - prepaid packages, safaris, cruises.

At Tesco's the choices are overwhelming. She spends a good half hour just walking through the aisles admiring what she could get if she had the money and so desired. The store has everything from brassieres to light bulbs to supposedly organic tomatoes. She does need socks, a new toothbrush, more Tabasco, bottled water and perhaps - cereal.

Instead she buys a liter of Baileys and a bottle of wine. A bag of carrots. Some hummus. Ramen.

Walking home in the dark, headlights looming towards her, cars whooshing past, she's not afraid. There's her cheerful flat with the enormous windows and high ceilings. Her little hideaway, all the more magical for the windy night.

Beyond that - and beyond the glass of wine she'll have as she responds to the barrage of emails in her inbox - there's Jake.

In Tesco's, he's sent her a text.

> Sweetpea, miss you already. can still smell you on me. xxx

***

She completes two edits that night, sipping wine on the bed, propped up against her pillows, her laptop balanced on the tops of her thighs, 'So You Think You Can Dance?' on low volume in the background. Cat Deely, the presenter, a familiar face. Makes her feel less hollow and alone, that first Sunday, in her studio.

Later, before she drifts off to sleep. Lying in bed in the dark. Thinking. Decides it's all about not looking down. As long as she keeps moving forward, walks the tightrope as if it's a line painted on the concrete. Then she'll be fine.

12.

From: jakepverse@hotmail.com
To: Mary Cartwright <scarymary666@yahoo.com>
Subject: evisceration
Date: Mon, 20 Nov 2006 11:13 am

Hey Mary,

So, I know I've said this before- but it's been QUITE some time since I've, er, snuggled or been snuggled up against. But- Oh, Mary, Mary. (Please know how hard this is for me!) I've wanted to tell you for some time, but then it always seemed like, this is crazy, this can't really be happening (you & me.) It's hard to know where I should start. I know we talked a little about this on Saturday night-

She doesn't remember. The whole night is still a blank. He could have told her he'd been in jail, won the Lotto, was married with three kids - anything - she'd be none the wiser.

I was telling you about my 'complicated situation' - how I live with an ex. You seemed pretty cool about it, but I don't know - maybe you were just being nice.

Mary's trying to channel herself, drunk, the other night. Trying to remember Jake telling her he lived with an ex. Can see herself giggling, batting an eye. If he told her - if it had sunk in at all - she would have at least dreamed about it.

Mary, please know you have NOTHING to worry about (it was over eons ago - and only lasted a millisecond to begin with! Now she has another boyfriend, they've been seeing each other for more than two years!) But here's the thing I haven't told you. And it's a doozy...We kind of have a son. (Yes, the Potter line has been perpetuated.) When my life imploded so dramatically the last thing I wanted was to fuck things up further by not doing right by the little guy. (Okay, so he's pretty darned cute. Yes, he's a ginger too - he's a

Potter, after all! Known as 'JJ' - Jake Jr.) So there you have it. Obviously the situation is not ideal (most of the time, if I let it, it can be downright bleak and miserable.) The three of us exist together in this house, but please believe me when I tell you that JJ's mother and I seek to exist as SEParately as the situation will allow. Fortunately she works, so weekdays I get the house to myself - I pick up JJ from his playgroup, and look after him until supper when my ex comes home and takes over. Weekends she takes him to her mum's, so she can frolic with her beau (that explains why my Saturdays have been so lonely. Until now...) Mary, I'm telling you this because I want to be completely open and honest with you. Most people know nothing about it (it's not exactly something one shouts from the rooftops!) My family doesn't even know! The set-up is so complex that I have found the most efficient means of coping is to banish myself to a non-feeling void. Also, I'm a non-confrontational type who just wants everyone to be happy- this means I tend to get knocked all over the place in striving to accommodate others. Oh Mary I am merely an angelic force in the universe. I mean no harm to anyone- it is not in my nature to hurt, take advantage, take for granted or abuse. I've just been so alone- and I'm so grateful to have chanced to meet someone like you! But I'm terrified this latest revelation will come as too much of a shock. If you would rather not take this any further, I completely understand. (And if you do- Oh Mary, I will most humbly offer myself to you...)

To Mary it all makes sense. Jake is a saint. She can't write him back fast enough.

From: Mary Cartwright <scarymary666@yahoo.com>
To: jakepverse@hotmail.com
Subject: Re: evisceration 12:08 pm
Date: Mon, 20 Nov 2006

Baby,

I love it. Its so weird- maybe I dreamed it- I feel like I knew? I didnt consciously know, but I sensed, and maybe thats why I never asked, though I'm not an asker. I like to let people be and share what they want to share. maybe because I have close friends in various states of similar deeply-connected-yet-not-type situations, I have to say, strangely, or not at all strangely, how cute! a little jake! he must be quite the rockstar...

Mary tries calling Vanessa, on impulse. She's pacing back and forth next to the steel desk, the ratty cord straining, nearly tripping her up when she forgets to lift it. Imagines Vanessa will now be more a fan of Jake than ever - and she was enthusiastic before, based on his picture and his poetry. But as a single mother, now she and Jake are linked in their struggles. Mary yearns to tap into that.

The line rings but Vanessa never picks up. Mary doesn't leave a message.

Soaring with Jake's revelations Mary has to leave the house. Spends the afternoon wandering through Didsbury Village on the pretense of shopping. Obsessing about Jake's ex. Pictures her plain because she has to - tries not to think about the last time they slept together. Years ago, she decides. Sees them sharing the very large house, occupying opposite wings. Tolerating each other for the sake of the boy.

Cutting through the park on her way home, Mary pays special attention to every small child she sees. Her whole life she's never been particularly drawn to them. Now she tries to guess their ages, looks for the ones who could be around four.

Back in the studio, she makes herself put away all her groceries before she checks to see if Jake has responded. All she wants to do is call him - but he never answers, and now she knows why. Surely he's read her message by now. He must know he hasn't lost her. Not by a long shot.

From: jakepverse@hotmail.com
To: Mary Cartwright <scarymary666@yahoo.com>
Subject: Re: Re: evisceration
Date: Mon, 20 Nov 2006 2:23 pm

Darling Mary,

You know, I sensed you would get it. We seem to have this connection that defies all logic. I ask nothing and expect nothing too- I'm a 'be and let be-er' (to be honest, I'm not much a do-er - I just am.) JJ is my special little buddy & that complicates my domestic situation. Especially as I've pretty much been the one left to raise him on my own. Btw, I wrote a poem about all this called 'Miracle Debacle' that you can find online. As much as I long to move out, I can't bear the thought of splitting his home. My plan has been to stick it out at least until the New Year. And he really is the most amazing little dude. Last night he fell asleep in my bed watching Zoolander! Mary, can I just say (again)- You are so cool...

From: Mary Cartwright <scarymary666@yahoo.com>
To: jakepverse@hotmail.com
Subject: Re: Re: Re: evisceration
Date: Mon, 20 Oct 2006 3:39 pm

jake.

if you could see the smile I have had on my face all afternoon. I think its fucking awesome. no wonder you are so wise...

***

'I'm living in Manchester.'

She's speaking to her mother at last. Something about Jake's revelation triggers a powerful impulse to reach out.

'It's so beautiful!' she's saying. 'Oh Mom, I wish you could see my flat. I can't even believe it - it's the most perfect place I've ever had.'

'That's wonderful, dear!'

'It's heaven Mom, it really is.'

Mary is making tea, adding three spoonfuls of sugar because these days she needs things extra sweet if she is to taste it. Everything inside her is moving at warp speed, so flavors need to be sharp or not at all.

Mary tells her mother everything, and her mother listens - that things are getting special with Jake, how great it is to get away from London for a bit, that Manchester is an ideal place to write, with lots of theater and small companies where she might workshop some plays.

'Jake says he might be able to hook me up,' Mary says. 'Who knows in the end, I'm here month to month.'

Only once does her mother slip.

'Do you know anyone up there, besides Jake?'

As she says it, both of them hear the anxiety in her voice, and both of them regret it.

'Of course,' Mary lies, laughing to hide her anger. 'There's a bunch of us - people I know through the whole theater scene in London. That's how I met Jake,' she continues, riding the brainwave. 'He's friends with friends of mine who live up here.'

'How nice.'

'It's great. Anyway, I better get going Mom, it was so great to talk to you.'

'You too, Mary.' Her mother says it with feeling. 'I love you.'

'I love you too Mom.'

Mary hangs up. Lights a cigarette. Stares out her window at the night. Wonders what Jake is doing. Wishes she could call him, hear his voice.

***

Before she goes to bed, she gets an email from Vanessa.

Date: Mon, 20 Nov 2006 10:44 pm
From: 'Vanessa Hope-Jones'
Subject: sorry I missed you
To: 'Mary Cartwright'

Darling,

Saw that you called & wanted to follow up just in case. You made it up there all right?

Well listen sweetie I want you to know we will always help each other because we are both nuts. Call me of course if you are ever in trouble. madcheater is a long call but can come up if needed.

Spent a lot of drug dazed days there as part of my ecstasy-addicted youth... was the best! Hard core you know the score! that was the madchester motto.

You need to understand that the north of england is a different place. Both my parents grew up in manchester. they are northern fuckers.

I think that the best combo is get the personality and talent from the north and get the fuck out to make money in the south....

but hey, i've seen the US

xo Vanessa

13.

'I just made myself a hot dog,' says Jake, over the phone.

'Yum!' says Mary.

They've slipped into a routine. Jake's first text always comes around nine. (Once JJ is safely delivered to playgroup, Mary assumes.) The next is at noon, when Jake gives her the green light to call. Mary has a landline; she always dials his cell. They talk for an hour or so - at first it's bits about their work, what they're having for lunch.

'How about you? Let me guess - something with Tabasco.'

'Yup. Sliced ham - with honey mustard too,' Mary says. Less than a month ago she was a strict vegetarian. Since high school, she never ate meat - with the exception of fish. Now in Manchester, she's frying up bacon, eating all manner of cold cuts, broiling filets. Craves it. Buys whole roast chickens at the market, pork chops, slabs of roast beef, even steaks.

'So, did you bake it yourself?' Jake teases.

'What - the ham? Are you nuts? Baking a ham is a serious undertaking. Did you make your hotdog from scratch?'

'No,' Jake is giggling. 'Picked them up from Morrison's. Oh - hey, wait a minute!'

'What?' Mary's finished the ham, wipes honey mustard from the plate with her finger.

'I think they came from America! The hot dogs.'

'No way.' Mary's thinking, really he bought them for JJ. But she won't bring it up - rarely do they talk about him. Maybe Jake mentions he's tired because JJ was up all night sick. Or that half-term is coming, meaning Jake will be unable to do the noon call. Not once do they discuss his ex. Jake might be living alone, the way he skips over her existence in his house. And Mary never brings her up - doesn't even know her name.

Mary lives for Saturday when she wakes at dawn - it's like the Britannia all over, the first day they ever met - the only twenty fours she wants to live. Might be her last day on earth.

No matter how much she's had to drink the night before, the butterflies are fresh and lively in her stomach. Leaps from bed as light and quick on her toes as a ballerina. Goes right to the kitchen and pours herself a glass of wine, sipping it at the counter with a cigarette - the first cigarette, the first drink - watching the sunrise, the birds already chirping, the light creeping up slowly, everything soft and golden.

This is it, she thinks. Knows anyplace outside the bubble she's in, her ritual would be dreadful. Knows she can't live this way forever - or even a few months.

But in the early weeks, those mornings at the counter with her wine and her cigarette, she is so happy and hopeful and calm. Is almost able to convince herself she doesn't need anyone. Even if Jake doesn't show up - doesn't come over ever again - it will all have been worth it, for this.

I'm sick, she thinks. But oh, what a sublime disease!

Chopping vegetables for the evening's meal might not be the most logical choice after a glass or two of wine at six in the morning. But it's her time, her treat. Thinks of the days, just after rehab, she spent working in the kitchen of a local café up the road from her mother's farmhouse in Massachusetts. A job she loathed and resisted at first, but grew to love. So that to this day, she often thinks maybe she would rather just wash dishes and prepare food someplace peaceful and quiet, where the folks are colorful and kind, and the land sweet-smelling and empty.

Her contentment in the kitchen makes her think perhaps she wasn't born lacking every domestic instinct. Maybe she prefers the life of a nomad to settling down, puppies and foals to human infants - but oh, how she loves to prepare food, especially for Jake. And fortunately, his wiry build betrays a considerable appetite.

He arrives at her flat Saturdays, after the football, when both of them have had plenty to drink. She's been eating all day the way she likes to - small tastes and nibbles to go along with glass after glass of the wine. Two bottles from six in the morning until Jake gets there in the late afternoon. Tries to keep herself to one, but it never works. As long as she's still standing, and the food comes out all right.

Thai lemongrass chicken is his favorite. Another time it's a Mexican feast - she even does homemade Jalapeno poppers - except she can't find Jalapenos and uses some other lethal strain. Both of them are so plastered by the time they settle down to eat, it doesn't matter. Only Jake breaks out in hives.

'You've got a heat rash,' Mary says, giggling, the next morning.

'Shit.' Jake is distressed. 'I guess I could say it's food poisoning.'

'It is food poisoning!'

Now Mary is the one with an uneasy feeling. The rash is on his chest - unless he's not wearing a shirt, no one would know.

***

The mornings after. Always hung over and on the verge of despair. But Mary holds it together, stays cheerful until he is gone. As long as he is there, or a text or an email away, with the promise of coming over, she's ok.

***

From: jakepverse@hotmail.com
To: Mary Cartwright <scarymary666@yahoo.com>
Subject: you reign
Date: Fri, 8 Dec 2006 10:24 am

Mary Mary Mary...

I don't know what it is that has thrust us together from the far corners of the universe (surely something more complex than Myspace!) It's as if I've been marooned on a very lonely, bleak island the last few years and you've paddled out to join me, making it a paradise. Seriously, I cannot believe my luck. I only wish I could spend all day every day nestled in your Didders lair - making food for you, ensuring you get plenty of bed-rest - heck, I'd even do your edits for you! Alas, for the immediate future all I can humbly offer you are my Saturday nights. (And for now, this arrangement could not be more perfect - from where I'm standing! To be able to spend even one night a week with you - well, I will take it!) Oh Mary - I adore coming to see you, the sound of your voice, your Tabasco fetish, the knee socks, your clover shaped bath... Paul keeps hammering me to come out with him but I don't feel like spending time with anyone else - am gonna blow him off (so to speak.) But Mary - I worry that maybe you are starting to feel a little like a princess in a tower? Already, this might be getting old, lonely or boring - you might prefer more glamorous nights out in madchester proper. or want to be left alone so you can do your brilliant thing with your play! what do I know? (only that I want to be with you any which way you'll have me, my badass American beauty...)

In truth, the weekdays spanning the time between Jake's visits are interminable. Mary fills them with edits. She exceeds all expectations, becomes a company darling, must wake every morning at four to get them all done.

As a consequence, the Friday nights before her long awaited Saturdays with Jake, she starts to slip. Allows herself a few drinks before she's signed off work for the evening.

***

'So... you're telling me I should open with a... with a film clip?'

The student on the other end of the line is somewhere in Baltimore USA. Mary hears the tightness in her voice, the frustration.

Mary is consulting with her over the phone, advising her on her application to PhD programs in psychology at Ivy League colleges like Harvard and Columbia. Giving her tips on how she should approach the essay - and Mary is drunk. She's drinking Bailey's, straight, over ice. It's the Christmas season, she's been telling herself. It's ten o'clock on a Friday night.

'Um, I'm sort of confused...' the girl says.

'No, really, it's thimple,' Mary slurs, and the jig is up. She's lost her. Mary is just some crazy person at the other end of the line.

'Um, hello?' says the girl.

'Hello, yes, Susie - STACEY,' says Mary, losing all traction. Trying to remember what the essay's even about. Is this the girl who works with autistic children? Oh wait, no, that was some other student. This girl is interested in suicide. Lost her best friend. Wants to be a psychologist, to work with suicidal teens. She's already an activist in suicide awareness. It says so right there on her CV, printed out in front of Mary. Smudged where her glass of Bailey's has sweated on it.

I have to get off the phone, thinks Mary. She's desperate.

'Hello? Hello?' Mary says, like she can't hear - like she's already lost the connection. And then she does it. She just hangs up.

A flash of panic. A moment of free-fall. What have I done? But the alcohol has taken hold. It will all be fine, the warmth tells her.

Smiling to herself, taking another healthy sip of Bailey's, she writes the girl an email. Composing on her own time, she regains control. She hopes.

> Stacey,
>
> My sincerest apologies. I am currently based in the UK and housesitting in a remote village in the North of

England. The phone service here is terrible - we were just cut off, and I have been trying to call you back to no avail.

I want to let you know that I am happy to continue working with you on your essay beyond what was stipulated in the guidelines of your 'Premiere Service' agreement. In other words, I am willing to edit your essay (and discuss it with you over the phone) until you are 100% thrilled with your piece.

Based on what we discussed this evening, I am going to go ahead and do another edit, which I will get to you before Monday. In the meantime, please do not hesitate to email me with any questions or concerns you might have.

Best,
Mary Cartwright
Editpro Essay Editing Consultant

She knows once she does her thing with the girl's essay all will be forgiven.

In the end, all that matters is Jake.

***

From: Mary Cartwright <scarymary666@yahoo.com>
To: jakepverse@hotmail.com
Subject: you rule
Date: Fri, 8 Dec 2006 11:19 pm

baby,

I'm just happy to be near you- even if it is several miles down the road and I only ever see you on saturday nights. that is a-ok with me. way more...
that is a gift.
really, I am just so happy you exist.

***

Except one time she lies.

Tells him she's going to meet up with friends from London who happen to be in town. Does it to make him jealous. This is on a weekday. A Thursday. A Thursday Mary is feeling resentful she can't just call him up and meet him at the pub like any other normal girlfriend and boyfriend might do.

She's sprawled on her bed, working on an edit and watching *Hollyoaks*. Ever since he tells her he once did a brief stint on the show, she never misses it - she's hooked. During the commercial break, she's restless, hungry, but she's not going to eat. Wants to call Jake, hear his voice - but knows he won't pick up. He never does, only when he green-lights her for the noon call.

Thinking about it, she's pissed. Has a little wine, a cigarette. Decides to send a text.

> Hey baby, just heard from •london friends who are in town - theatre folks - you'd love them. On my way to meet them at a pub. Come join us! Please? Xo

Stands there in her kitchen, in her sweatpants and socks. He texts back immediately. Even this is extraordinary. Between the hours of three and half seven or eight he's usually incommunicado. The digital clock on the stove reads six forty-five.

> Hey Mary, that's great! Have fun- wish I could join you xojtp

Now she's really angry. He's so detached, so distant. She watches the rest of *Hollyoaks*. Chops some vegetables and eats them with hummus. Finally an hour has passed. She texts him again.

> yikes! I think I;m a little drunk. At this cool place on •oldham street.oh baby, wish you were here. These three guys are hitting on me. argh!

That gets him. He starts drinking at home.

> baby, I'm jealous! Drinking vodka. Where are you now?

Mary is drinking too. Now she has his attention, she's working, sipping wine. Every hour or so, she texts him like she's at another bar, a lounge, a club.

At one in the morning she's in bed, finishing her last edit. Texts him she's finally headed home.

That night, for the first time, he calls her. He's a little drunk, a little frantic.

'Baby! You made it home all right?'

'Yea. That was fun.' She's still angry, wants to punish him.

'I wish I could have come.'

'Yea. Me too.'

'So those guys were cool?'

'They were awesome.'

'Your friends from London? I want to meet them.'

'Yea, they're leaving tomorrow. Next time.'

'Maybe this Saturday we should go out - Paul's still hounding me.'

'That guy doesn't like me.'

'Why would you say that? Mary, he thinks you're great.'

'He does?'

'You don't remember? That time we all went out. The two of you discussed plays for hours.'

'We did?'

'Yea,' Jake chuckles. 'You don't remember? He said I should hang on to you.'

'Really?'

'Yup.'

'I guess I'd be up for going out Saturday,' she says, although she doesn't really mean it. She still wants Jake to herself. Doesn't entirely believe him about Paul.

But she's tired. She feels better. She knows he cares.

'Jake, I have to go to bed.'

'Me too. Sweet dreams.'

'Night, baby,' she says.

***

Saturday she meets him at a pub in the village. The game starts early, at half twelve. Mary spends the morning trying to decide what to wear. Settles on her tartan, a black bustier, and a sheer low-cut jersey top. Because really, it's all she's got - aside from her pink pants, now starting to get ratty and worn.

And she drinks. By the time she calls for a car to take her to the pub on the village green, she's already seeing things in flashes. Bottle of red wine, empty and teetering at the edge of the counter. Crushed cigarette pack fallen on the floor. Her lips, freshly blotted with red lipstick.

Takes a car because she's not going to walk or ride the bus. Not going to go through that again - all the old ladies staring.

The pub is low-ceilinged, has shuttered windows, diamond shapes criss-crossed in iron. Feels like she's stepped back in time - Chaucer's era and she's the Wyfe of Bath. Jake likes to tease her about the gap between her front teeth. He calls it a diastema. 'They say it's a mark of Venus,' he tells her. 'A woman who's highly sexed.'

'Oh great,' she says.

It appears out of nowhere. She notices it when she moves to Manchester. At first she tries to get rid of it. Sleeps with floss wrapped around her teeth, holding them together. It works but it's painful and when she unwraps them during the day, the teeth splay back apart. So she gives up. The gap grows and then stops. Living unofficially in a foreign country means no dental or health care.

The birth control pills, however, are easy to get. She does it after her very first weekend with Jake. Figures he already has one child he didn't plan. She wants everything to be easy for him. In the Yellow Pages, she locates a women's center just up the road.

The waiting room is dingy and worn - nothing but chipped browns, outdated pamphlets on the side tables, magazines from another century. *Woman's Day* from 1998. Mary imagines she's in a Mike Leigh movie.

She fills out a form and when her name is called, she follows a nurse up two flights of stairs to a tiny room. They don't even examine her. Just take her blood pressure and ask a few questions.

'Do you smoke?'

'No.'

They give her a four-month's supply - and it's free.

When she tells Jake she's gone on the pill he seems embarrassed, shy.

'Um, okay,' he says, blushing.

Four months will see her through April. An eternity.

At the pub Jake reaches his little pinky out and links it with hers. They're standing by the bar. The game is on the big screen, Manchester City versus Manchester United. It's a City crowd. Jake's team.

He gives her a quick sideways look and she glows. Could stand there forever like that, secretly linked to her sweet man. Sneaks glances at him, his elegant pale features, his thick red hair. He's looking at her, too, between plays.

This is enough, she thinks. This is all I want, this is perfect.

***

Halftimes and quarters. Commercial breaks. Mary slips to the loo. Wanders through the pub on her own. Jake is somewhere - in conversation with people he knows. He's introduced her. She remembers this, vaguely.

Paused in corners. Standing near strangers, enormous men - red-faced and smiling. An overweight woman with peroxide blonde hair. Hideous orange carpet. Place filled with cigarette smoke, more bodies, blue jerseys. Pints everywhere. Bubbly ale in clear glass mugs, spilling over. The crowd at the bar. Bartenders pulling pint after pint.

The game seems to last forever but Mary remembers very little of it. Manchester City loses, three to one.

They stay at the bar.

The rest of the night is in snatches.

Jake flushed, affectionate, his arm around her. Talking fast, with gusto, about meeting Paul in town at a club.

The cab, and Mary paying as it's pulled over on a city street. Bills raining out of her wallet like petals off a dead flower.

The club. Two floors and she's sitting at a table, speaking intently, passionately to Paul.

People are dancing to Bob Dylan. Mary's in the downstairs bar now, talking to someone important - another playwright? Jake smiles at her from across the room.

She's buying drinks. The man she's been speaking with is looking at her strangely. Her bustier top has slipped down, her small breasts exposed. Without blinking, without pausing in her conversation, she pulls her top back up.

At a table of strangers. Now she's in the upstairs bar again, off to the side of the dance floor. Fumbling for her jacket - it's not on the back of the chair, not under the table. In the dark, barging into groups of people, asking if they've seen her stuff. Crawling under tables, searching the floor.

Jake has found her, holds her tight. They are in a corner, kissing in the dark.

'I love you,' he says.

'I love you too.'

'Let's get out of here.'

'I lost my jacket.'

'Let's just go.' He takes her hand and leads her through the crowd, down a flight of stairs, past bouncers, out onto the street. Jake grabs her face and they kiss on the sidewalk. Wind whipping, it's biting cold. Cabs streak by.

She pulls away. 'I need my jacket. It has my keys, my wallet!'

Now they are pushing past the bouncers again. How they get back inside is a miracle of drunken determination. They just do it.

She goes to three different tables, feels the backs of the chairs, people get up, she crawls on the floor, down by their ankles. Where is it?

On a bench lining the far wall of the dance floor, she goes to it like she's known it was there all along. Her worn pea coat with the lining coming loose in the back. Holes in the pockets but not big enough that her wallet, phone or keys will fall out. Not yet. And it's all there.

Mary and Jake, whooping, hands in the air sail down the stairs once again, one last time, victorious. In the cab careening towards her studio, money spills out and Jake is sucking on her earlobe. Now they are kissing, she is in his lap.

Now they are pulling up the drive to her building, and it's a good thing. They are home.

***

'We made pizza?' Jake says the next morning. He pads from the bathroom back to the bed, in his boxers and grey socks.

Mary sits up, looks around. 'Apparently we did.' A large plate is on the floor near the bed, nothing but crusts on it. 'I guess we were hungry,' she smiles.

Jake climbs back in bed with her. 'You were drunk.' He wraps her in his arms.

Mary giggles, but deep inside she's a little terrified. Remembers nothing past arriving at the Horse & Jockey, snatches of the game, looking for her jacket at the club.

'You were great last night. I looked over and you were talking to one of Manchester's most eminent poets. You didn't know it but your top slipped down. Standing there flashing your breasts, totally oblivious.'

'Oh my God.'

'Then you saw. Pulled up your top without missing a beat. It was fantastic. Paul and I watched the whole thing.'

'I don't want to know.' Mary's burrowing down deep, gone under the covers, clinging to Jake's side. 'Baby, hold me,' she whispers. The world has gone stark. It's tipped with a jerk and she's trying not to panic.

14.

Mary finds the meeting online. Just down the Wilmslow Road, at half twelve on a Tuesday. Clears a place in her edits so she's able to slip away. Leaves the flat at eleven, to give herself plenty of time.

Only she has her doubts as she walks over there. What will she tell Jake? What will they do - what will they talk about, if she isn't drinking?

Plenty, she tells herself. Shame pushes her along. No more topless spectacles in nightclubs. No more waking at dawn in a cold sweat. Wetting the bed. Blackouts.

Still, she gets lost. Can't find the right building. By the time she figures out where it is the meeting has started. From where she's standing outside on the sidewalk, she can see in. Only three or four people, and they all look hideous - fat, seedy. Smoking, staring dull-eyed at the floor, at the wall.

Mary turns on her heels, and flees.

***

After her father dies, when she goes to rehab, she's actually looking forward to it. She's ready, she needs a rest. It's a relief. Mostly it's twenty-eight days she can grieve. They even switch her to the trauma track; she spends mornings beating up chairs with giant bats made of foam. She never even knew she was so angry.

Family Week sees her start the process of reconnecting with her mother. That is harder. Sometimes it's easier to make peace with those who have died. In life her father could be brutal, but now he is gone, Mary can love him unconditionally, without being scared of what he might do or say.

But her mother is still there. The fact she shares Mary's loss, Mary's love for her father, makes everything worse. Mary resents her.

'I feel like it wasn't even about me,' Mary tells her. She and her mom are sat face to face in chairs, the rest of her group looking on. 'You told everyone I was a drug addict. Like I was this monster.'

'Honey, I was terrified.' Her mother is crying. 'I kept thinking every time the phone rang, it was going to be someone telling me you were dead.'

'Oh my God.' Mary is so disgusted she has to look down. The rage in her gut like some grotesque creature, clawing to get out.

'I love you so much.' Her mother is sobbing openly now. 'Your father was dying. I couldn't bear to lose both of you.'

At this Mary cracks. The hole she's been lugging around, the vast chasm of missing her dad swallows her up, so she's choking, breaking down. 'I'm so sorry. I miss him too...'

In the months that follow, she leaves New York, moves into the farmhouse with her mom in Massachusetts. Takes the job in the kitchen, at the local café. Hatches the plan to go to graduate school in England. Her mother isn't thrilled, but Mary applies anyway.

'Honey, why the UK? Why not choose something around here? Brown University has an excellent program. You always loved Trinity Rep.'

'Mom.' Mary hates explaining anything, once she's made her mind up. 'Studying in England - it's always been my dream. You know that. My God. Studying plays in London! There's the National! The Old Globe! It's where I want to be.'

'How will you afford it?'

Mary takes out student loans when she gets in. Flies to London to start her course in September. By February, she's drinking again.

She never makes a conscious choice, it just happens. She's out with her classmates at the College Arms, where they usually go on a Tuesday after their three-hour workshop. That day they're discussing Sarah Kane, Mary's hero.

'I would have given anything to see *Blasted*, at the Royal Court,' she's saying.

'The show the *Daily Mail* called 'a disgusting feast of filth'?' says her classmate Dave.

'Yes! Awesome,' says Mary. 'Pinter got her. I love that.'

'You know next week is the anniversary of her suicide?' says Ellen, the class know-it-all. Bearer of bad news. She's also the only one with an agent.

'I'm getting another round,' says a guy named Ben. Mary's favorite, the youngest on the course. His work reminds her of Albert Innaurato, raw and off-the-wall. 'Mary, another Diet Coke?'

They don't know she doesn't drink. Maybe one or two suspect it.

'You know what?' says Mary. 'I think I'll have a pint.'

'Great.' Ben turns to go to the bar. No one else bats an eye.

Mary has three. The afternoon bleeds into evening. By six o'clock she's soaring. The others are ready to leave. Out on the sidewalk in front of the pub they say their adieus. Mary waits, pausing to light a cigarette, but mostly, she's waiting for them to go.

Back in the bar, she meets a group of Australians. They start doing shots. Inside she feels rotten to the core. But with each drink she gains momentum, soon she's indestructible. They stay until last call.

Next a club in Soho. The Australians are gone and she's with two men who might be Danish. Brittle blonde, gaunt faces, skin stretched over bone. The three of them snorting cocaine off the tabletop until a bouncer escorts them to the street.

She doesn't think twice about sliding into their cab.

'Come to ours for a nightcap, eh?' says one, his eyes half shut, stares out at her through slits.

They're shooting down Commercial Street, potholes smashing. This is where I live, Mary thinks, but doesn't say it.

The other guy is caressing her thigh. It doesn't feel right, but the thought of going to bed now, alone, without one last drink to take the edge off feels worse.

'Yea, okay,' she says. 'I'll stop by for a quick one. Do you have any weed?'

They sit in the flat in the dark. At first they might have beers, be sitting one on the couch, two in easy chairs. Then one of the guys is tapping out lines on the coffee table.

'Oh no way,' Mary hears herself saying. 'I'm done.'

'No, no-' says the one on his knees, now rolling a note. 'Ees not what you think. This is better, here.' He hands her the tube and Mary takes it. She's tired, too tired to resist.

'It's Ketamine,' the guy is saying at her ear. All she knows is it doesn't burn like coke. Once she gets past the overwhelming urge to vomit, it's all right.

All three of them are on the couch. Mary is topless. Watching one guy hold her arm up, he's admiring it; now he licks her, wrist to armpit. She feels nothing. The other guy is at her breast. Feeding like a baby.

The light is changing in the room. Mary's been staring at the ceiling. Now she's aware of the body on top of her - and one below. She's naked and it hurts.

Mary starts, her whole body jerks. An arm yanks at her neck. Mary cries out, something knocks her in the head. She's frantic, struggling now, thrashing with all she's got. The blows come steady, her neck caught, now she cannot breathe.

Flash of white and everything quakes, goes dark.

Broad daylight, but still early. Mary opens her eyes. A scratchy blanket covers her. The flat is empty. She wants to sob, but her face is numb. Throbbing. Nose drips blood.

Finds her clothes, her wallet, phone and keys. Inside she's whimpering. Slips out the door, a cab stops for her immediately.

'71 Commercial Street please, right before Petticoat Lane.' Her voice is raw and hoarse. The driver nods, says nothing. Just keeps looking at her through the rearview mirror.

When he pulls up at her address she goes to pay him.

'Nah,' he waves her away.

'You sure?'

'Take care,' he says, speeds off.

She falls asleep soaking in the tub, and when she wakes, the water is cold and brown. She stands under a hot shower, waiting, thinking nothing. Bundled in her bathrobe and a towel she crawls in bed and sleeps for hours.

Maybe it's the next day, or a day later. She walks into a meeting at Toynbee Hall. All she has to do is cross the street from where she lives. She doesn't talk, doesn't take in anything. Her face is bruised, but still she's clean, well dressed.

'My name is Emma,' says a woman afterwards, as she's leaving. 'Would you like go somewhere, have tea?'

Mary nods.

They find a little Turkish place off Brick Lane. Sit and drink mint tea for hours. Emma's face is gentle, she doesn't say much, just nods as Mary talks, and holds her hand. It's nearly midnight by the time they part. Emma walks her home.

'You have my number,' she says. 'Call me anytime.'

'I will,' says Mary. 'Thank you.'

And she means it. Even if she never calls, never responds when Emma texts and calls her in the weeks that follow. Never goes to another meeting.

Drinks, but carefully. For dear life.

15.

'I may not be able to come over next Saturday.'

'Next Saturday is the day before Christmas Eve.'

'I know. I'm sorry baby. My aunt is coming to town to see JJ, it's going to be hectic.'

'Oh.' In her head, Mary thinks, aunt? And, I thought you said nobody in your family even knew?

But she doesn't bring it up. 'Maybe you could come over Sunday?' she says instead.

'Christmas Eve?'

'Yea.'

They are in bed. She's wrapped around him, he's sitting up, holding his coffee, trying not to spill it.

The idea of spending the long stretch from Christmas Eve to New Year's Day alone in her studio with nothing but edits is something Mary is starting to dread. Not like the year before, when she was alone. It was different, she wasn't in love. Housesitting for Vanessa, who was off skiing in Verbier. London at Christmas was exhilarating and magical. She wandered the quiet streets in awe. Walked through Hyde Park and started to think maybe she really did believe in Jesus and God. The ducks on the chilly water, the mist coming off the lawn. Cheerful tourists. Everyone so nice on Christmas day. The peppermint mocha from Starbucks never tasted so good.

'Yeah. I could maybe do Sunday.' Jake kisses her on the head.

'What about your present,' she says at last.

'Uh oh. What about it?' He's tickling her a little. She giggles. Has a vision of what he must be like with JJ. Sometimes it feels like he's humoring her in the same way. Bribing her with kisses, going down on her - instead of coloring books, instead of candy.

She's bought him tickets to the Morrissey show at the Palace. Only the show is on a Friday, a taboo day, and she's afraid he won't be able to go. Maybe she does it on purpose. If he can't come it will give her something concrete to rail against.

Now Jake reaches down and grabs her feet. He knows they're one of her most erogenous zones. So much so, she can hardly stand to have anyone touch them. Pedicures have always been out of the question, unless she gives them to herself.

'Baby stop.' She squirms even as he strengthens his hold. Now he's straddling her, grips her toes.

Oh, she thinks. What she would give for him to pull off her underpants right now.

Instead, he holds her feet up, grinning down at her and she stares right back at him, this boy that she loves. They stare intensely into each other's eyes a lot, because often there's nothing to say. Or too much. So much between them must remain unspoken.

Except now, she takes a deep breath, dissociates from her feet. She's going to broach the subject because it's Sunday and the show she's spent two hundred pounds on is less than a week away.

'Baby, I need to give you your present.'

'Now?' He has no idea, and even though he's feigning disinterest, he's like a little kid, he can hardly wait.

'Kiss me first,' she says.

And he does. Slowly, he leans down over her, his strong slim body. Still gripping her feet so she might cry out at any moment. The kiss is stupendous. It's hard to stop. Only he pulls away.

'Okay, what is it?'

'Hang on,' she says. 'I need to get up.'

He releases her feet and she's off the bed, sprinting to the kitchen where she's hidden the tickets under the bottle of Bailey's on top of the fridge.

She doesn't need to turn around to know he's grabbed his phone. Always when her back is to him, he checks for messages, then slips it away like it was nothing.

She takes down two envelopes. One holds the concert tickets, and the other is an early Christmas gift from her mother, a pair of Marks and Spencer's gift certificates, fifty pounds each.

Mary holds the tickets - it's all right there. *Front Row. Seat 4. Morrissey. December 22nd. Palace Theatre. Manchester.*

Now she reconsiders. Something in her gut gives her pause - realizes she doesn't have the nerve to be let down. Not yet. Instead she takes a gift certificate, folds it in her palm.

'Ba-by?' Jake says, dragging it out slow and scolding, like she's done something wrong.

'Don't look. I want it to be a surprise.'

It's a relief for both of them. Jake sets his coffee down, covers his eyes. Mary darts to his man bag. Pulls the top book out - Maurice Blanchot's *Thomas the Obscure* - and replaces his Oxfam bookmark with the gift certificate. Slips the book into the bag and zips it.

Once she's back at his side, he strokes her head. 'Baby,' is all he says, quietly, under his breath.

It's like he's on the verge of saying something - what it is she doesn't want to hear.

'Jake?' She can't help herself.

But he surprises her. Always. Instead of bringing up something unknown - something she dreads - he kisses her. Slowly, gently. It is the softest, sweetest kiss. And in it she forgives him whatever it is he hasn't been able to say, knows he loves her.

Once he's gone, she crawls into bed, deep under the covers. Falls asleep and dreams they're on a boat together. A large ferry, perhaps a party barge. It's some kind of celebration, they are out at sea and the night is beautiful, the water gleaming. Jake keeps smiling at her, squeezing her hand. And then of course, they get separated. Mary can't find him. She's searching everywhere, growing frantic. Yet deep down she knows he's gone. Begging strangers, have you seen him? Where is he? She's a nuisance, shameless, feels everyone's disdain.

***

From: jakepverse@hotmail.com
To: Mary Cartwright <scarymary666@yahoo.com>
Subject: xmas etc
Date: Tues, 19 Dec 2006 2:35 pm

Hey yo!

Baby, good news! it looks like I may manage to sneak away on Saturday after all! But the thing is (bear with me darling...) It's going to mean accompanying my ex to the Morrissey show Friday night (she bought tix as an xmas gift - Mary, I was SHOCKED. Believe me when I say we have not spent time in each other's company on a harmonious, non-little-goon-known-as-JJ-related level in YEARS - around 4 to be precise!) But this would free me up to be with you on Saturday. What do you think? Okay, so the prospect was not to me initially pleasing - made me rather queasy, in fact. Even wracked my brain for feasible excuses (lies!) but in the end methinks it best I accept my fate. Am def going to lose sleep over it, but see no alternative-

Tonight must meet Paul and an old friend of ours (from the early days of the 'revolution'!) who is crazy for the ladies (meaning I have a long night of sleazy bars, short skirts and strip clubs ahead.)

But I shall soldier through the grim lot of it, knowing I'll soon see you - Saturday, as always, I hope...

Sitting at her desk, Mary is paralyzed. Already the montage has started in her head. Jake and his nameless, faceless ex in the lobby of the Palace, holding hands. Packed in amongst the crowd, standing together - she's leaning against him, whispering in his ear. They're grinning, laughing. A couple that's been together for years. Relaxed together. With a child at home. They are a family.

And after the show? They go home together. Drunk. Kissing. Send the sitter off. The Christmas tree is in the living room. Check on JJ, sleeping like an angel. Falling into bed together.

Mary is nauseas but can't stem the thoughts. She has no control, except to leave.

But she can't. She's not ready to give up, to let go. Not yet.

***

Later, after many silent laps around the park in the cold - walking it all off, walking it all out. When she feels calmer, vigorous in her body, refreshed and clear. Still angry, still desperate to hang on to him.

> From: Mary Cartwright <scarymary666@yahoo.com>
> To: jakepverse@hotmail.com
> Subject: Re: xmas etc
> Date: Tues, 19 Dec 2006 5:46 pm
>
> jeesh.
>
> well that email just filled my heart with xmas cheer. sorry.
>
> maybe hit me at a bad moment- i.e. cooped up thousands of miles from friends and family on christmas doing nothing but stanking edits.
>
> sorry sorry. but this made me cry.
> and now I must run-
> to prepare for another stupid edit phone call.

The rest of the evening Mary works. Tries not to think about Jake out with the boys, in strip clubs or even gay nightclubs, with Paul. It's bad, but she knows it will be worse in three day's time - on Friday, when he's out with his ex, seeing Morrissey. Determines to keep her head up. Finds solace in her clients. Something she can depend on. Pours her soul into each essay, and her clients respond.

Subject: Thanks
From: alexkang@vt.edu
Date: Tue, Dec 19, 2006 9:29 pm
To: mary_cartwright@editpro.com

Dear Mary Cartwright,

I do not know how to thank you enough.

Your corrections are so powerful but at the same time beautiful that I could even fall in love through the essay.

My hands are almost shivering as I type and I just wish I were better in expressing my thoughts to show enough of my gratitudes towards your work.

Thank you so much again.

Alex Kang

***

It's a few minutes past midnight. Mary has just switched off the light to go to bed when Jake calls.

'Baby!' he blurts when she picks up. The way he's breathing, she can tell he's drunk. And she's dead sober – starved herself of alcohol in her sorrow, for a change.

'Jake, where are you?'

'City Centre.' She can hear him walking, the wind muffling the sounds. 'Looking for a cab.'

'Oh.' Mary's turned on the light. Heads into the kitchen, reaches for the bottle of red wine above the fridge.

'I made my escape,' Jake confides. 'Lost them at some gentlemen's club. Paul already ditched us for Gay Village. I miss you.'

'I miss you too.'

'Hang on. Can you call me back? I'm running out of minutes.'

'Sure.' Mary calls him back from her landline.

'The whole night I couldn't stop thinking about you,' he gushes. 'Oh wait – there's a cab!'

'Get it! Don't take the bus.'

'I'm not - one sec-'

Mary downs a glass of wine and pours another as Jake sorts out his ride. Feels like herself again. Everything is going to be all right.

'Come over,' she says, when Jake returns to the line.

'Oh Mary. I want to. You know I can't.'

She does. But then again, she doesn't.

'Mary?' Jake is whispering. 'You still there?'

'Yes. I'm here.'

'I love you,' he says.

'I love you too.'

Even though they've said it once before, on the mad night out with Paul, somehow it feels more earnest and real this time. Even though Jake's drunk. It's Christmas.

'Stay on the line with me,' he says.

'I will.'

She stays on the line with him until he gets home, stays with him as he makes a piece of toast and eats it. Is still there as he takes off his pants, and lies down.

Stays with him until he falls asleep.

16.

From: Mary Cartwright <scarymary666@yahoo.com>
To: jakepverse@hotmail.com
Subject: re: re: xmas etc
Date: Wed, 20 Dec 2006 8:49 am

baby, was so amazing waking this morning to your gentle breath in my ear.
(okay, so let's not think about my phone bill!)
jake, I'm so sorry - I need to come clean about something-
remember last sat - when I wanted to give you your xmas present? well. you see. really I got you something else. (the m&s certificate was from my mom)
actually I had tickets. to Morrissey.
I wimped out giving them to you then- I wanted to surprise you, but I guess I also knew you probably wouldn't be able to go.
Oh, but I was hoping. Ah well.
I am a dumbass.
so sorry sorry sorry- the whole situation shouldnt have bummed me out so. I'm just burnt out on the edits is all. I have everything to be grateful for.
you most of all.
baby,
I love you.
I wont ever doubt you.
I trust you.
ms. doofus

***

'You have no idea,' she's telling Guinevere. Cooking ramen on the stove. Adds two eggs, her mobile gripped in the crook of her neck.

'Tell me about the little boy. Is that weird? Have you met the mother, his ex?'

'He's beautiful.' Mary coasts directly into lies. It feels so natural, so good. 'Jake's amazing with him.'

'He's three?'

'Four. A little Jake - a ginger too! JJ. He's completely obsessed with Jake.'

'Oh my god. So you've met him? You guys are pretty serious?'

'Well, I guess so,' Mary giggles. 'I don't know, we'll see.'

'What are your plans for New Year's?'

'You know, I'm not sure.' Mary takes the noodles off the stove. Lets them sit. 'I think we might stay in. What's going on in London?'

'Oh you know, the usual parties. Darling, I miss you. But I'm so happy you're happy.'

'You have to come and visit!'

'Oh my God, I'd love to.'

'You and Nigel!'

'For sure. Maybe sometime in spring, May or June?'

'That would be awesome.' Something sticks in Mary's stomach. In May the editing season will be over. Her income will be gone. 'I miss you too, you know.'

***

The Morrissey tickets remain atop the fridge. Once Jake can't go, Mary keeps thinking she'll sell them. Post an ad on Ebay, or Gumtree. Even toys with the idea of going despite him - to spite him. Imagines getting all dressed up, going out to the City Centre on her own. Hitting the pubs until she finds someone really hot. A guy as wily and fierce as Jake - one who is thrilled to be with her, who will see her on any night of the week. Who will answer the phone when she calls.

She imagines she will meet this other, and they will go to the show. And Jake will see them, with his dumpy partner, and be gutted. She wants him to suffer.

Because Mary, the night of the show, suffers. She doesn't go out. She has edits to do. She drinks too much wine. Cries. At her drunkest moment she decides she's had enough, determines to leave Manchester.

She imagines calling Guinevere, Vanessa - even her mother. Breaking down, telling them everything. Hears them taking her side, offering sympathy. Offering to help her. Insisting she come home.

Mary wants to text Jake, but by nine-thirty she knows the show isn't over. Probably just started. Her head swims with wine and she can't even get up to fetch a glass of water.

Passes out fully clothed, on top of the covers. All the lights and the TV still on.

***

When she wakes at first light, her throat is dry. She's sickly with hangover. Remembers the Morrissey show. That Jake was there with his ex. Reaches for her phone, sees he hasn't texted or called.

Her head is thick but she's sober. Slips from the covers, places her numb feet on the hardwood floor. Has coffee in silence, with a cigarette. Watches the sky turn from pink to gold to a bluish-grey. It's going to be overcast. Looks like snow.

Maybe it's the caffeine, but something lifts inside her. Jake gave his word, he's coming to see her. She trusts him. He will be there in only a few hours. It's the day before Christmas Eve, she has the whole glorious morning to herself.

Now she's buzzing. Tingling with glee. Bundles up, dumps the rest of her coffee in the sink, and steps out into the early morning - filled with optimism and an open heart.

***

'There's even something for you!'

Jake is warm and in the flesh. Has only three hours, but they're making the most of them. Mary has brought the box of Christmas gifts from her mother to the bed.

'Check it out,' she says, unsealing it, tearing open the flaps.

Jake leans over eagerly. He's naked, pale hips barely covered by the sheets.

No matter how bereft Mary might be during the week, their lovemaking always sets her straight. For the next few days or hours at least.

That afternoon especially - Jake must know. Feels the tenuousness of their thread, frayed by the holidays. He takes his time with her. Goes so slowly Mary thinks she's going to burst.

'Here.' She's perched in bed beside him, on her knees, the cardboard package opened between them.

'You want me to do the honors?'

'Yes.' Mary runs a finger along his shoulder, her favorite part. The vulnerable curve beneath his ear.

'That tickles.'

'No way!'

'Here, silly.' Jake is pulling out tiny presents wrapped in colored tissue paper.

'Wait. I should open the card first.' Mary pulls out a large envelope tucked in the side.

> Darling Mary, Merry Christmas! It's not much (everything was selected by weight. I wanted to be sure they arrived on time.) Hope you have a wonderful holiday! I love you so much, Mom.

'Aawwww,' says Jake.

Mary kisses him on the nose. 'She's cool, my mom.'

'You guys are close?'

'Sure. Look, this one's for you!'

He takes the flat package from her, feels it. 'Hmmm. Something soft.' Reads what's written on the front.

Jake, to keep you warm. Merry Christmas! Susan

'Go on. Open it. I want to see what she gave you.'

Jake unwraps the red tissue. A blue and white striped scarf.

'Nice!' Mary rises up on her knees, wraps it around him. 'Handsome.'

'Yeah?'

'Yea.'

They open the rest of the gifts. A bag of peppermints. 'These were my dad's favorites.' They each take one, sucking them as they go.

A pair of gloves. 'To keep Mary warm.'

Dried apricots. Trail mix. 'She likes to know I'm eating healthy.'

Three pairs of the softest socks. A wooly hair-band. Godiva chocolates.

The care package now empty, there's not much else Mary can do to keep him there. As if on cue he sighs, 'Tomorrow's Christmas Eve. I should get going.'

'JJ must be so excited.' Mary's strangely ebullient now. 'Jake, it will be great,' she continues. 'C'mon.'

She's rallying him; inside they're both surprised.

'I hope you're right,' he says. 'I'll try to call. It might be hard-'

'Baby,' she's kissing him. 'I understand.'

Packs the mints, the apricots, the trail mix, in his bag.

'What are you doing?' he asks.

'For you. JJ's stocking.'

Jake shakes his head. Now he's dressed, ready to leave. 'Thank you, Mary.'

'Thank *you*,' she says.

Something strange happens as she's talking to her mother later that night. Sitting there, her place all brightly lit, TV on for company.

'Honey, you know they finished the sculpture for your father.'

Her mother has had a special memorial made. A fish cut from stone, meant to go down by the stream at the bottom meadow on her parents' farm.

'I want to see it,' says Mary.

'I know. It's going in next weekend. I'll take some photos and email them.'

'No,' says Mary. 'I really want to see it - to be there.'

'Oh.'

'I could come the last weekend in January. Be there for the 26th.'

They both know the date. It hangs in the air.

'Would that be okay?' Mary asks. 'If I came back for a couple of days around then? I need to leave the country and re-enter anyway because of my visa.'

'Oh honey,' her mother says in a tiny voice. 'I would love that.'

'Cool.'

'Let me pay for your ticket.'

'Mom. You don't need to. I can afford it. And hopefully Jake can come too.'

'You'd be bringing Jake?'

'Yea, well. We'll see. He doesn't like to leave JJ for very long. But if it's only for a few days…'

'My goodness! The end of January - it's just a few weeks away.'

'I know. Oh Mom, I hope Jake can come. I can't wait for you to meet him!'

***

She doesn't have to wait long for the right moment to ask. It happens New Year's Day. They are flushed, drunk, chasing after each other on the streets of Chorlton at dusk. Man City has beaten Everton two to one.

It's Monday, but a holiday, and Jake calls her just before the game is to start. The whole thing is unexpected and wonderful. Mary drops everything to meet him at the pub. So happy, so delighted he wants to be with her for the big game, on the first day of the year.

Ducking out of the pub after too many pints, wanting only to be together, to laugh and to kiss. Along Beech Road Mary steals his wool hat, darts behind a dumpster, the newsstand. At the corner she races into a phone booth. Jake catches up to her, slips inside and closes the door.

'I've got you now,' he says, pulling the hat down over her ears, pressing into her.

'You do.' She runs a finger just inside his waistband, tempted to do more. It's almost dark enough.

Jake reads her mind. 'Hey, we don't want to get arrested.'

'Come home with me,' she says.

'Right now? Yea, maybe I could.'

'Come home with me.'

'What?'

'I'm going to my mom's at the end of the month. Come with me.'

'Really?' His face is so close to hers, their noses are touching.

'Just three days or something. I'll pay for your ticket. You won't have to do anything. Just show up at the airport.'

'I've always wanted to go to America.'

'You've never been?'

Jake shakes his head. 'Nope.'

'Then you have to come.'

'Really?' Jake is grinning now. Excited. Hugs her tighter, they kiss.

17.

Because Jake implies he might be able to go with her, it's all Mary can think about. In her head she's already given him multiple tours around the small town in Massachusetts where her parents have a farm. They've tramped through the fields, stood by the brook where her father used to fish, napped in the afternoons on a creaky four-poster bed laden with quilts.

Jake is coming over weekdays now. Arriving by noon for lunch, a blowjob, a walk through the park, then catching the bus back to Chorlton.

Mary has started buying little treats and toys for JJ. First it's candies, sweets - then crayons, markers - a fancy coloring set.

'Mary, this looks expensive.'

'It wasn't. Picked it up at Lidl. Isn't it great?'

'It is pretty cool. But… It's going to seem like I've taken up shoplifting.' Jake takes the shiny plastic case from her, examines it. All manner of paints, stencils, sheets of construction paper inside.

He shakes his head. 'JJ is going to love it.'

Mary beams. 'So Jake.'

'Ye-es.' He knows what she's going to ask. Less than two weeks, Mary's flying home. He still hasn't given her an answer.

'Um. So do you think you might be able to come?'

'When do you need to know by?' Jake is scratching his head. Looking at her sideways. The fact he says this gives Mary a new spurt of hope.

'Wednesday?'

Jake has the coloring set under his arm. It won't fit in his bag. He holds out his hand. 'C'mon sweetpea. I should get going.'

'What time do you have to pick up JJ?' Mary can't believe what she's just asked him - and it was so easy!

'I need to be there by three. But I have to prepare. Make sure I have the right food, DVDs. Enough to keep him busy so he doesn't destroy me.'

'Yea,' Mary giggles. Like she knows.

They are outside her flat now, cutting across the park. She's picturing Jake and JJ together, walking home from school hand-in-hand. Wondering what JJ sounds like. When she will meet him.

Mary sees Jake off at the bus. He waves to her once he's taken his seat on the top deck, in the front. The best spot, like being on an amusement park ride.

That afternoon, Mary sees it in his eyes - he's not coming. But the way he goes along with her plan, as if he might still be able to go, touches her. Makes it okay.

***

One Saturday he brings her pictures of his family. He's come from the pub, they're both tipsy.

He spreads the photos out before her, pointing out his relatives. His late mother, his cousins, the aunt who came to visit at Christmas. Mary knows she'll remember each one.

'That's your mom?'

'Yea. That was taken on my birthday. I think I was twelve.'

In the photo a young Jake stands grinning beside a woman who makes Mary think of a deer, or a gazelle. So tall and slender. With Jake's pale eyes and fair complexion.

'She's beautiful.'

'Yeah. She could have been a model. She had offers, but she met my dad. He was a rugby stud at the time.'

Mary wants to ask him more about how she died. He's talked about it before, but she can't remember. They were drunk at the time. It was some kind of cancer, like her father. Jake was in his teens.

'Oooh, let me see that one,' she says instead, reaching for a photo of his parents on their wedding day. 'Wow. So handsome.'

'Yea, they were really in love.'

'You can tell.'

Mary tops up their wine. Kisses Jake on the cheek.

Much, much later. They are in bed, Jake is asleep. Mary slips out the covers and darts into the bathroom. Coming back, she pauses at the photos on the counter. There's one of JJ, dressed in a cowboy costume, for Halloween. Another of Jake's mother. She's sitting in an old-fashioned parlor with a cup of tea, in conversation with someone beyond the frame.

Hello, Mary thinks as she stares at the photo. You have a wonderful son.

***

When Jake finally tells her the next morning he can't go, it's a relief.

'You know I wish I could...'

'It's okay,' she says, kissing him. 'I understand.'

He pulls her close. 'Tell me more about it though. I want to hear.' He's nuzzling the hair at her neck, squeezing her side. 'Your mum's house is in the country?'

'Yes. It used to be a weekend place. My parents always lived in Boston until my dad was called to Washington.'

'Sounds like a spy.'

'Nope. Just a lawyer. But a good one. The best.'

'Tell me about the farm. So, do you have horses?'

'Not anymore. Just dogs. They're like my mother's children. She even cooks for them on the stove.'

Jake chuckles. 'Your mom lives there alone.'

'Yep.' Mary is staring up at the ceiling. Wonders what her mother would make of Jake. 'I can't wait to see her.'

'I do want to come.'

Mary rolls over, considers his face. 'Jake, you'll call me though?'

'You'll be gone just the weekend, right?'

'Yea. Wednesday to Sunday. But I'll want to hear your voice.'

Jake sighs, reaches a hand to her face and trails his finger along her cheek.

Mary's luggage consists of her knapsack. Leaving her flat at dawn, she pauses at the door and takes in her studio. Everything neat, put away. Standing there, she can't help thinking, what if this is it?

She takes a car to the airport. It's still dark out, the sky shot through with purple. As they hit the motorway the horizon is simmering orange. By the time she steps out in front of the terminal it's a dull grey. More drizzle.

With more than three hours to spare, she has to wait for the check-in desk to open. When it does she's the first one through.

The guy looks at her passport and raises his eyebrows. 'January 25th, your visa expires. Cutting it close.'

'What? Let me see.'

The man hands her her passport.

'Wow. I had no idea.' She hands it back and he stamps it.

'Thank you for visiting Manchester. Have a safe flight.'

She keeps checking her phone, hoping for some kind of farewell text from Jake. Wanders the duty free. What to buy him? Then she remembers her mom and selects a giant Toblerone.

Only when the plane is seconds away from take-off does she turn off her mobile, after she caves and sends him one text.

> Darling, I'm off - will catch you on the other side. Xxooo

Tries to sleep on the plane, but she can't. She doesn't drink either. Too great a risk. Still, she can't read, can't work, can't stop her feet from wiggling under the seat in front of her. Watches a bit of the film - Almodovar's *Volver* - but all she can think of is Jake's crush on Penelope Cruz. Listens to the 'Relaxation Meditation' track on her iPod - but it's no use. Nothing holds her focus. She just wants to be there.

As the plane lands she is shocked to see so much snow. Forgot how frigid and icy January in New England can be. Manchester seems tropical in comparison.

Turns on her phone. Jake has sent her three texts.

> Baby, safe flight! I wish I was with you xxx

> Sweet thing, just found the money & note you stashed in my bag. Naughty. But much appreciated.

> Little goon & I eating pizza - tried to make from scratch like yours. Fuckd up the crust - JJ thinks its good tho☺ will txt you tomorrow when to call - love to yr mom!

***

Mary's mother is waiting for her at the international arrivals gate.

'Oh honey-'

'Mom!'

Mary hasn't even put her bags down, her mother is hugging her.

'You look wonderful.'

'So do you.'

She's smaller than Mary remembers. Feels her bones as they embrace. Mary's afraid they might snap.

'Mom,' she says. Blinking back tears, giggling to chase them away.

On the way to the car, through the long plate-glass passageways, everything is grey concrete. A still winter's day. They walk in silence. Barely twenty minutes after their reunion, Mary's hopes for connection are ebbing away.

She waits until they are in the car, then asks, 'How are the dogs?'

Her mother perks up. 'Oh well, you know.'

Mary doesn't, but she can guess. Her mother hates to leave them, even for the two hours it takes to get to the airport and back.

'Truman must be so big now.' Her mother's German Shepherd, just a puppy when Mary saw him last.

Her mother's eyes sparkle. 'He is, but he's still a big baby.'

'And Ralph?' Ralph is Mary's favorite. Her father's dog, the chocolate lab.

'Oh you know, he's hanging in there.'

Ralph is ancient. Mary's relieved he's alive, that she will see him. They've always had a special bond.

'That dog's an ox,' she says, and both Mary and her mom look down. Know what the other's thinking - that her father was an ox too. Or should have been.

In the car her mother turns off the book on tape that comes on the minute she starts the engine. Jane Hamilton's *When Madeline Was Young*. But the silence is too much.

They get as far as the highway before Mary says, 'You can turn the radio on.'

Her mother obliges, both of them relieved. A country folk station, Linda Ronstadt singing 'Desperado.' After only a few bars, Mary finds it excruciating. But she keeps quiet. Decides to make another stab at conversation.

'So everything's good?'

Her mother turns to her, surprised. 'Why yes - yes it is - why do you say that?'

'No, I just mean, you're well?' says Mary, flustered.

'Yes, Mary,' her mother says, eyes on the road. There is a tightness in her voice and Mary can sense something has shifted - and what's worse, she prompted it. But neither of them says anything.

Johnny Cash comes on the radio, and Mary starts to relax. Looks out the window. Thinks about what Jake might be doing.

Back at the house everything seems smaller. A little bit run-down. Her mother's not as neat as she remembered. There's dirt on the windowsills. A funny smell in the kitchen. Dog hair everywhere.

'Shall we go to the brook?' her mother says, after Mary has put her knapsack in what used to be her room, now a guest room. All her riding trophies, horseshow ribbons that once lined each wall long stashed away in boxes. Old clothes, notebooks, dolls and random jewelry neatly packed away in the basement. Only to one day be thrown out, Mary thinks. She will be the one to do it.

Like her father's things. All his clothes sent to the Salvation Army. Mary kept a set of cufflinks. Photos her mother doesn't even know about - her parents on their wedding day, one of her father when he was at Yale, relaxing in an easy chair in his dormitory, smoking a pipe.

'The brook?' Mary says now, lingering at the kitchen sink. 'Oh, right - to see the fish!'

Her father had admired the sculpture in a magazine. Talked about having one made, just like it. Commissioned a local artist. Only he never lived to see it. When it was finally completed, they couldn't bear to pick it up and bring it home. Not until now, nearly four years later.

'Is it out there?' Mary asks.

'It is. They installed it last week, right before it snowed.'

'Let's go then.' Although secretly Mary wishes she could go alone.

Because she's packed light she doesn't have a winter jacket - only her thin pea coat. Mary contemplates the selection in the hall closet - down parkas, rain macs. Her father's hunting coat.

Seeing it, she's swept up in a burst of anger - doesn't quite understand it. Except, she's thinking, how could they miss it? Her mother must have set it aside. Wanted to keep it - but why?

Mary's rage is sudden and irrational. It's all she can do to keep from marching through the hall with it, into the kitchen. She's burning to confront her mother. 'What were you *thinking?* Why would you keep this? *Why?*'

But she remembers to breathe. Counts down slowly from eight, like the therapist in rehab taught her to do. She has to do the countdown three times, but it works.

'Honey, you coming?' her mother calls out from the kitchen. She's all ready to go, bundled in her full-length parka, hunting cap and mittens. The dogs whine at her heels.

'Yea, Mom. Just a sec.'

Mary reaches for the coat. Feels the soft suede, the heavy lining. Lifts it off the hook, and slips it on. The whiff she has of her father is overwhelming. Yet she's surprised - she's comforted, not dragged down.

Her mother doesn't say a word about it when Mary joins her in the kitchen. Just pauses for a moment, taking her in. Sniffs, pulls her gloves on tighter.

'Right then,' she says. 'Off we go.'

Mary smiles to herself; the way her mother says it, she might be English.

They tramp through the back fields in the snow, the dogs leaping like seahorses the drifts are so high in places. The only sound, that of their boots plunging through the icy crusts - and the seagulls overhead, the brook in the distance.

Mary remembers the day she was finally able to cry, months after her father died. She was home helping her mother sort through his stuff. Had to take a break. Walked out across these very fields on her own, and broke down. Her face chapped with tears. Wailing at last, the wide-open space obliterating all sound, so that no one could hear.

They reach the hidden curve in the brook, where the pool is so deep even on the sunniest days it's black. Finally, Mary feels she has come home. The fish sculpture takes her breath away.

'Oh Mom. It's beautiful.' Reaches for her mother's gloved hand. Squeezes. Her mother squeezes back.

'Isn't it?'

Her mother's smile is serene. She looks stronger, more solid, and Mary is relieved.

They stand there for a bit, hand in hand. The dogs crashing through the underbrush all around them. Listening to the birds, the water rushing cold, clear and fast through the break in the rocks.

Gazing at her father's fish, carved in a green-tinged stone - Mary so warm in his coat, like he's holding her.

Hey Dad, she thinks. Here we are.

18.

'So tell me about Jake,' her mother says. She's sipping a glass of wine at the kitchen table while Mary cooks dinner.

'He's an amazing father.' Mary is on her third Diet Coke, trying not to stare at the way the moisture is condensing on her mother's glass. The Sauvignon Blanc is perfectly chilled.

Curled at her mother's feet, the dogs follow Mary with their eyes. She's grinding meat for a bolognese. Ralph is drooling.

'You've met his son?'

'Oh, yes,' Mary lies, and as she does so, she knows her mother can tell.

'Just be careful, honey,' her mother sighs.

'What?'

'You know - when there's a child involved. It can be complicated. His ex knows you've met the little boy? She's okay with it?'

'Sure,' says Mary, looking down as her face gets hot. Slowly working the hand crank as she feeds the last piece of tenderloin through. Dumps it all in the hot skillet to brown. 'They haven't been together for years, she's totally cool with it.'

'So you've met her too?'

'Oh yea,' says Mary. The meat is searing, steam billowing up from the stove. She wipes a stray piece of hair from her face with her wrist. So far in the deep end she's resigned to drowning.

'Anyway, Mom, he's great but we're taking it slowly, okay? We're both adults, jeesh.'

Mary dumps the meat in the bolognese. Sets the water on to boil. Takes the fresh pasta from the fridge and places it on the counter.

Time for a cigarette. What she would give for a glass of wine.

Instead she removes her apron, goes for her father's hunting coat. Her Marlboros are in the pocket.

'I'm going to step outside real quick. Get some air - take the dogs out.'

Her mother smiles. 'Thank you for making dinner, Mary.'

'Oh my God - Mom. It's my pleasure. I cook for Jake all the time.'

'Well, it smells delicious.'

'I hope,' says Mary, grinning. Slips out the kitchen door, the dogs tumbling after her. Walks carefully across the ice on the back porch in the dark.

Stares out into the night. No stars, only a slip of a moon.

Hugs her father's jacket tight around her, breathes in his scent.

'Oh God,' she says under her breath. Then, 'It's all good. It's going to be okay.'

The following morning. On UK time, Mary is up well before sunrise. Lies in bed, waiting for the light to change. Past four-thirty, five. At five-thirty she gets up, creeps out into the living room. Startles - her mother is there in the easy chair, wrapped in a duvet. Her spectacles on, a book balanced on the armrest.

'Mom! You're awake,' Mary whispers.

Truman and Ralph gaze at Mary, perched like slovenly sphinx's on either side of the hearth. Eyes enormous, hopeful. Big tails thudding on the rug.

'Morning sweetheart,' her mother smiles.

'You slept out here?'

'Well,' her mother says.

Mary can see she's embarrassed, and immediately feels guilty. 'No, no, it's okay. I can see why, I mean, its so cozy out here, with the fire.'

Her mother just smiles, folds her book and slides it between her body and the chair cushions. It dawns on Mary that this is where her mother always sleeps - and has for some time.

When Jake texts at seven-thirty, her mother is in the shower. The house is a small cape, so even if they are in separate rooms, there's not much privacy. Mary rushes into the bedroom with the phone and shuts the door. Dials his cell.

'Hey,' she says when he answers.

'You made it.'

'I did.'

'What time is it there?'

Mary looks at the clock on the wall. 'Twenty to eight. Not so early. You having lunch?'

'Just coffee.'

'Not hungry?' Mary can see him in mittens, hands wrapped around a mug of instant.

'Well. I'm nervous. Come to think of it, the caffeine is probably a bad idea.'

'Maybe not. Might be like Ritalin for hyperactive kids.'

'Huh?' Jake is distracted.

'You know - it's a stimulant, but it chills them out.'

'The coffee is definitely stimulating me. Hang on, I'm gonna dump it.'

Mary can hear him moving from room to room, he must be wearing boots. Somewhere a siren. 'Jake?' she hesitates. 'Why so nervous?'

'Oh - didn't I tell you? I have an audition.'

'That's great! What's it for?'

'This show Paul is directing. At the Exchange.'

'Paul Baggot?' She says his name and her voice actually cracks.

'The one and only.'

'I still don't think he likes me.'

'Why do you say that?'

'I don't know. It's a vibe.'

'He thinks you're great.'

'Yea, right. Whatever. So you're auditioning today? What's the show?'

'*A Fair Country.*'

'Oh my God, I love that show. Jon Robin Baitz. I saw it in New York at Naked Angels when I was young. My dad took me.'

'It's great, right?'

'Fuck, that's awesome.'

'I know,' Jake says. 'I should get ready. Baby, how's your mom?'

'Yea, she's good.' Mary peers out the window. A dainty pair of titmice feed at the suet-log suspended off the back porch. On a patch of ice below a large crow watches, head titled. 'I miss you.'

'I miss you too.' Jake says it cheerfully.

'Text me later,' she says, trying to sound just as casual. 'Tell me how it goes.'

'I will.'

'Love you.'

'Love you too.'

Mary hangs up the phone. The house is quiet. Her mother has finished her shower.

She lies down on the bed and sleepiness creeps in like a tide. Only she's kept awake by thought of Jake with Paul - and her not there.

The visit goes better than expected. She and her mom adopt a routine, a manner of communicating that works. It involves not pressing too deep, approaching gently, leaving lots of space.

At night in the guest room, Mary can't sleep, tries to keep her mind a blank. Not cave in to wondering what will become of her. In the presence of her mother, her lies and the truth take on an ugly weight. Also being sober night and day.

The Friday night, Mary's last. She and her mom have just finished dinner - the leftover spaghetti bolognese, and Mary's baked an apple pie. Unofficially celebrating her father's birthday.

Mary is clearing the plates, scraping leftovers directly into Truman and Ralph's bowls. Her mother is taking out the ice cream, sets the fancy dessert dishes on the table.

Mary's cell phone rings, shrill and loud. Truman and Ralph perk up and Mary's mother raises an eyebrow.

It's Jake.

'Hang on Mom, sorry.' She darts out of the room, into the hall, down to the bedroom. Closes the door, conscious of how late it must be where he is - already in Massachusetts its half eight.

'Hello?' Mary says, answering the phone. 'Jake? Hello?'

All she hears is loud noise - a crowd of people, music, shouting. A general, steady, uproar. It dawns on her Jake hasn't called her - his phone has. And he's out on the town, in a lounge or a pub. At one-thirty in the morning.

'Jake? Jake, hello?'

But it's no use. Mary hangs up. Hesitates. Dials his number. Does not expect he will pick up, and he doesn't. Waits for his outgoing message, the beep.

'Jake, hey, it's me. I think your phone just called me. Silly. Sounds like you're out having fun. Love you. Okay, bye.'

Mary hangs up, but still she feels uneasy - feels awful. Heads back out to her mother, the pie and the ice cream.

At the table her mother sits, brow still raised. 'Everything okay?' she asks.

Mary wants to hit her. Then she feels guilty, riddled with shame. Ice cream, she tells herself.

'Yum,' she says to her mother. 'Everything's fine.'

They are sitting, eating, not even two or three minutes later when Mary's phone rings again.

'Crap! I'm sorry Mom, I thought I turned it off-'

'It's okay honey, go ahead, take it.'

'You sure?' Mary asks, but she doesn't even wait for her mother to nod yes. She just leaves, hurries back down the hall.

'Hello? Hello?' she says, once she's back in the guest room. Again, no Jake on the other end, just the sounds of a pub or a lounge. A cacophony of voices, laughter, shouts. A female voice now discernable in the mix, Mary's sure of it. And Paul's voice, it has to be.

'Jake? Jake pick up!'

Nothing. Mary clicks off again, it's hopeless. Now it's nearly nine. Two in the morning where Jake is. Wherever Jake is.

Mary returns to the table. Her mother, she notices, hasn't waited. Her pie is all gone, she's licking the last bits of ice cream from her spoon. Mary feels ill, has lost her appetite. Sweets, ice cream in particular, now seem especially nauseating. But she can't do this to her mom.

'Have some more,' she says to her mother, handing her the Haggen Daz carton.

'You know what? I think I will.'

'Good,' Mary smiles. Considers her slice of pie, now in a creamy soup of melted vanilla. Thinks, what I would give for a glass of red wine. A shot of whiskey. Would that were Bailey's in my bowl.

Her phone rings again.

'Oh Jesus, Mom, I'm sorry!'

Mary waits for her mother to say it's okay. But this time she doesn't. Only looks up, taking a large mouthful of ice cream. All Mary can think is how it drives her crazy the way her mother eats. The sounds. The smacking.

Without another word, she leaves yet again. Sequestered in the bedroom, she answers the phone.

'Hello?'

'Mary?'

It's Jake. He's slurring, drunk, but all there.

'Baby!' she sighs. Sits on the bed, the phone pressed to her ear. 'Where are you?'

'Not sure. Outside some club.'

'You went out?'

'Yea, me and Paul. Hey, I got the part!'

'Jake, that's awesome!'

Mary can hear him walking now, he's breathing hard. She imagines him making his way down a cobble-stoned street, someplace down by Gay Village, for some reason.

'I'm drunk,' he says.

'Yea, I can tell.' But she giggles to let him know she doesn't mind.

'Stay with me,' he says.

'Of course.'

And she does. Even though she knows her mother is out there, abandoned at the dining room table. She doesn't go back. She can't. She can't leave Jake. Drunk and wandering around alone on the streets of Manchester. Nearing 3:00 a.m.

Like the time before, she talks him home. He gets in a cab, gives the driver instructions to his street in Chorlton - the first time Mary hears his address. The first time she has any inkling where he lives. With JJ and his ex.

While she's on the phone, she can hear her mother moving around. Now she's in the kitchen, doing dishes, putting things away. Hears her talking to the dogs, hears the door slam as she takes them for a walk.

Jake has made it home. Talks him through the decision of whether or not to have some toast. 'Baby, you should eat something - you're going to be hungover.'

But he's too drunk. 'Too much of an operation,' he says.

Hears her mother come back inside with the dogs, the water running in the bathroom as she brushes her teeth, the flush of the toilet. Imagines her bundled in the duvet on her chair in front of the fire. Maybe she's reading her book. More likely sitting in silence.

Talks nonsense with Jake as he bangs around his house. He's drunk but chatty. Stays on with him, past midnight her time. When they finally hang up Mary turns out the light, pulls up the covers. Doesn't leave the room to brush her teeth or wash her face. She will wait until morning. Knows her mother is probably waiting too.

19.

In the airport before her flight, she has three Bloody Mary's. Sits in the dark bar, the fire returning to her belly. Her foot wiggle is back. Talks to the guy sitting beside her.

'Yea, I live in Manchester.'

'Manchester? Like Manchester United - John Beckham!'

'David Beckham. Yea,' Mary giggles.

'You a student?'

'Oh no. No.' Mary hesitates. 'Moved there to be with my boyfriend.'

'Ah. Lucky guy,' says the man. He's what one would expect to find in an airport bar. A generic type of salesman in a suit. Maybe he said he was in marketing for Dell. Mary's not sure but she's tickled he might have been flirting with her.

On the plane she drinks two of the tiny bottles of red wine and passes out before the meal even comes. Seems like she's just closed her eyes and then opens them and already they are preparing to land. The orange juice in the little plastic container makes her stomach hurt. Does her best to tamp the pain by forcing down a few bites of the cardboard muffin.

Only when she stands up to exit the plane does she notice she's still a bit drunk. Everything is vaguely spinning and unbearably stuffy as she waits in line to go through Immigration.

Thinks nothing of it when the tight-faced young woman asks for her passport.

'So you left Manchester on Wednesday. And now you're back.'

'Yep,' says Mary, smiling. Not bothered - aware she might reek of alcohol. The red wine - she's swallowed a gob of toothpaste, brushed her teeth. Curses herself for not buying Altoids when she had the chance.

'Ah...so you've been living here?'

Something in the tone of the woman's voice gives Mary cause for concern. That and the fact she's waving two other immigration officials over.

'Well no - I mean, I was - I was a student - but now I'm just visiting-'

'You left the country on January 24th - but before that you'd been here six months - as a visitor. How have you supported yourself?'

'No, no - I'm still just a visitor - I mean, I work, but not in the UK-'

'I'm sorry, but I don't think we can give you leave to enter.'

'What? I don't understand - no, please-'

There might be a trapdoor where Mary is standing, suddenly opened up and she is falling, flailing in a white-hot panic.

The woman has turned to the two other officials who have joined them.

'What seems to be the problem?' says one.

'No visa - she's been here as a visitor-'

'But working?'

'Well, that's what we're getting to.'

'Step over here Miss.'

Mary's in a sweat, feels it damp on the back of her neck.

'We need to see all your paperwork.'

'Yea, yea, sure, of course!'

Mary's in a side room now with the officials, the door is closed, but at least it's a little cooler. Spots a red phone mounted on the wall. Will she be asked to use it - to book her flight home? Call Jake? Or her mother?

Her knapsack is ripped open on a table, her things spilling out. Rubble of clothing - jeans, knickers, socks. Floating on top, her passport, lip balm, receipts, checkbook and a stack of envelopes. Bank statements and pay stubs. Her mother gives them to her before she goes. All of it gets mailed to her mother's address. A miracle, she has them.

Mary tears at the envelopes, victorious. Sees her way out.

'See - see - I work online - it's a US company…'

The officials are gathered around now.

'Okay,' says one. 'So you haven't been employed in the UK.'

'No. In the US - I'm traveling - I can work and travel - it gets direct deposited - see?!' Mary pants.

'Right.'

'Let me have a look.'

'Right, okay.'

'How long are you planning to stay in Manchester?'

Mary gets it. Finally. 'Just one week - then I'm going to Spain.'

'Spain?' says one of the officers.

'Yea. I have cousins there.'

'Do you have your ticket? Can we see it please?'

'Ah, no. It's online, not printed out yet.'

They all know it's a lie. Mary's about to give up, hangs her head. Waits for the inevitable. No leave to enter.

Silence. Glances exchanged above her head.

'Okay,' the woman who first stopped her says at last. 'You're leaving in a week? Right?'

'Yes! Yes, I am,' says Mary.

'Next time be sure you have your return ticket.'

'I will, oh I will!' Mary's shaking, gathering her things. Mad to get out of there. Have cigarette.

'In the future, if you only have a one-way ticket, you won't be allowed back in the country, just so you know.'

'Thank you,' says Mary. 'Thank you. I'll remember.'

***

Home in her studio, Mary keeps the shades drawn, the lights off. Crawls in bed. Home safe.

Her phone on the chair next to the bed vibrates. Jake. Phoning her, not just a text.

'Hey,' she says.

'You made it.'

'Barely.'

'Barely?'

'They almost didn't let me back in. I can't talk about it.'

Jake giggles on the other end.

'No, not funny. Terrified. Baby, please come over.'

'Yea?'

'Please.'

Falls into a coma sleep. When she opens her eyes, Jake is standing there.

'Hey,' he whispers. 'The front door was open. Your door was unlocked.'

'Please, come hold me.'

Without a word, he removes his pants, his shirt. Slips under the covers with her. So warm, breathing in tandem. Holds her tight.

***

That Saturday they drink far more than usual. No football match, so Jake comes over early. It's still light out. Afternoon. They start in on the wine.

By six o'clock they both are slurring. Order Indian food, only to eat a bite or two. Neither of them is hungry. Start kissing, shove it all to the floor. Make messy love.

Fill the clover-shaped tub and take a bath, clothes strewn across the studio, the hallway. Splash water everywhere, the tub overfull. Great puddles on the floor.

Later, wrapped in towels, on the bed. Mary clings tight to his chest.

'I was so scared.'

'Shh. It's okay,' he says, stroking her hair.

'No, it's not.'

'Shh.'

'Jake.' She's angry at herself, for the tears - she's crying. Just plain angry.

'It's not okay,' she says with too much force. 'I'm going to run out of money. The edits stop in another month or so. I can't work, I'll have to leave the country.'

'Shh. We'll figure something out.'

'What am I going to do?'

'Shh. There, now.'

'I have nowhere to go, I have no home.'

'Baby, yes you do.'

Mary pauses, almost doesn't dare to look. Then peeks up at him. 'I do?'

'Yes,' he says. 'With me. I'll always be your home.'

'Oh my love.' Rests her head, at last. They lie there, just breathing. Mary's heart thuds - her mind won't be still.

I want I want I want.

Sees the wine. Gets up and pours them each a glass. 'Cheers,' she says with a grin.

'Cheers.'

They both drink. Mary takes their empty glasses, sets them down.

'Baby?' she asks. Crawls towards him on all fours. Both of them naked, the sheets slipped off the bed.

'Yes, sweetpea?'

'Um, I don't know how to say this...' Now she's straddling him.

'What is it?' He's stroking her thighs.

'Well,' she says. 'I mean, there's one way I could stay here. But it's kind of major. For you.'

'Mary,' Jake says. Smiling now. One hand steadying her at the waist. The other ever stroking, up the inside of her thigh. 'Should we get married?'

'Oh, Jake-' His finger is inside her, takes her breath away. 'I mean, it would just be for the visa. I could pay you even-'

'Don't be stupid. I'd do it for you. I don't give a shit.'

'I don't believe...,' Mary says, coming down slowly on his fist- '...in marriage either.'

'Baby.'

'Jake,' she sighs. 'I - do - love - you-'

20.

'I'm fucked.'

Mary's pacing the studio, triumphant. On the phone with Vanessa.

'Oh Jesus,' Vanessa sighs.

Mary can picture her in her fancy flat. Opening the bedroom window, placing a glass of expensive red wine on the sill. Preparing to have a covert cigarette.

'Okay,' says Vanessa, inhaling now. 'Explain to me the situation.'

'Oh my God. So we're getting married. But it's mostly for my visa. I mean, I love him, and I hope we'll be together forever. But you know, who needs a piece of paper?'

'Right, unless you need to stay in the country.'

'Correcto!' says Mary.

'So I don't get it. How are you fucked?'

'Well, no. I'm not really, but it's a bit of a precarious situation. You see, it's not just my visa. I haven't paid my student loans since September.'

'Mary! It's February!'

'I know I know.'

'What about your taxes? You're paying them in America, right?'

'Um, not for the last three years.'

'Jesus, Mary. You are fucked. But I guess if you don't ever go back-'

'Yea, well that's the thing.' Mary's lighting a cigarette now, crossing to the kitchen. Grabs a dirty mug from the sink to use as an ashtray. 'I did some research and I actually have to fill out all this paperwork and get this fiancée visa from the British Consulate in New York.'

'O-kay.'

'Do you think they'll check? I mean, are they going to know what a financial mess I'm in?'

'Honey, I have no idea. But bureaucratically speaking, if the British consulate in New York is anything like the administration here, I'd say you'll be all right.'

'Yea. It's also gonna cost a fortune. It's like five hundred pounds - plus I have to fly to New York.'

'You need some money?'

'No, I'm good. Been working like a banshee the last six months and I have a nice bit saved. But I will run out of money if Jake and I don't get married soon and I can get a job.'

'Well let me know. When are you thinking of tying the knot?'

'I guess it depends when I get the visa. Sometime in April or May?'

'Exciting! Oh Mary, when you have the date, tell me, I'll try to come.'

'You could be our witness!'

'And June.'

'And Junie!'

***

Time passes quickly when the only thing that matters in a month are four Saturdays. Marrying Jake is all she can think about. Only they don't discuss it. She means to talk about it further, pin him down. Wants to desperately every time he comes over. But something holds her back. Fear he won't remember. What if he's changed his mind? She doesn't want to know.

***

She's shopping in Chorlton. The Oxfam bookshop has the best selection. Finds a massive Jean Rhys biography - one she never knew existed.

'Jesus, that should keep you going,' says the clerk when she hauls it to the register.

It's a Wednesday, early spring and sunny, warm. Mary takes her book, buys a mocha, heads over to the village green. Half three. Jake is in rehearsals for the play. It opens in a week.

Mary sits along the low stonewall. The children have just been let out of school and the grassy expanse before her is teeming with them. Wobbly midgets all tearing about, squealing, falling down. At the far side of the green, the mothers and nannies and babysitters with their prams and colorful bags.

Though she's some distance from melee, Mary's having trouble reading. One child in particular has caught her eye. A little redhead dressed in overalls, with chocolate on his face, a wild look in his bright blue eyes.

It's him, she thinks.

Instinctively she knows it's JJ. Can't take her eyes off him.

Is it him? Or not?

For one crazy moment she has an impulse to text Jake. And say what? I think I see JJ in the park?

Nearby she spots his sitter, a teenaged girl with streaks of pink in her blonde hair. Chunky black shoes and shredded leggings.

'JJ,' the girl calls out. 'Five more minutes.'

Holy fuck. It is him. Mary looks down. The girl must be Jenny. Jake has mentioned her before - 'You've met our sitter. Yes, you have,' he says to her one morning a few weeks back.

'No-'

'Yes, the night you lost your jacket.'

'Oh my God.'

'Don't worry. It was before your top fell down. She thought you were cool. When you weren't looking she gave me the thumbs up.'

When Jake tells her this, it reassures Mary more than he could know. Not that his sitter likes her - that Jake is okay she's seen him with Mary. Like it's all out in the open. Everything's cool.

But now Mary's nervous. Doesn't want to seem a stalker. Hides her face behind her book, can't stop peeking. JJ's still racing about, giggling. Already he moves just like his father.

Several yards away, Jenny stubs out a cigarette. Calls to him, 'JJ, time to go.'

'No! Noooo - look!' He's making like an airplane, whirrs towards her before tumbling to the ground.

'C'mon you,' says Jenny. Helps him up, a firm grip on his pudgy hand.

'Noooo-'

'Honey, yes. Let's get you cleaned up. Guess what I have for you...'

Now their backs are turned, their voices fade. Mary watches as they walk away, headed towards Beech Road and all the shops.

Once they have disappeared from sight, Mary stands to leave. Clutching her massive book to her chest she walks slowly to the bus stop. By the time she gets there, she's resolved not to say a word to Jake. When she plays out the scene in her head where she tells him, he's alarmed.

***

'Mom, I have something kind of major to tell you.'

'Okay...?'

Mary takes a breath, bursts out with it. 'Jake and I are getting married.'

She doesn't plan to bring it up, it just spills out. Maybe hearing her mother's voice again weakens her defenses, softens her, clouds her judgment. They haven't spoken since they last saw each other - maybe exchanged some emails.

The silence at the other end of the line is ominous.

'Mom?'

'I'm here, honey. Wow,' her mother says at last.

'I know,' says Mary, before her mother can say anything else. Already something inside her is spiraling down. It's too late. She knows she's made a grave mistake.

Keep it simple, she tells herself. 'I'm so happy, Mom. I really love him.'

'Oh Mary,' says her mother. Then she surprises her, 'Honey, I guess...I'm happy for you.'

Mary's caught off guard for a second. Now flushed with warmth, she wants to hug and kiss her mother, feels so close.

'Oh my God. Mom! I'm so glad. I can't tell you what that means-'

'Darling, of course. Have you set a date?'

'Um, I guess soon. We just want to do it quietly, at City Hall.'

'Well let me check the flights.'

'Huh?'

'I'll plan on coming out there, shall we say, in two week's time?'

'What?'

'To meet Jake. You know, I think brother George has something in London soon, maybe I can coordinate with him. I'm sure he'd love to see you too, be a part of it all.'

'Right. Yea. Okay.' Mary sits. 'Sounds great.'

***

Sunday morning, they're lying in bed, fabulously hung over. Jake's play has opened. The *Manchester Evening News* calls him 'winning and tormented' as the radical young journalist Alec. Mary's hopes are bolstered at the thought of her mother and Uncle George seeing him on stage.

'So baby, when my mom is here next weekend?'

'She's coming to see my play?'

'Yep. She'll be there for closing night, Friday.'

'What if she doesn't like me?'

Mary hits him in the thigh. 'Shut up. She'll love you. But you can come out to dinner with us Saturday night?'

'Urrgh,' Jake moans, rolling over. Pulls a pillow over his head. 'I don't do parents.'

'Baby, please?'

'Do I have to? I'm going to see her Friday, right? Saturday should be the two of you. You don't want me. Besides, there's the football match. No way I can miss it.'

Mary's trying to stay calm, casual. 'When does it start?'

'Half six, I think.'

'Well, we won't eat 'til late. Baby, please?'

Jake sighs, rolls over facing her. A wry smile. 'I'll try.' Kisses her on the nose before getting out of bed. Disappears into the bathroom.

Mary waits. Doesn't say anything at first when he returns. Watches him get dressed, prepare to go.

Finally she says, 'So, um, Jake?'

'Yes?'

'I told you how I went to rehab and all that?'

'The first night we met.'

'Wait, I did? Oh my God.'

'You don't remember?'

'No, no. I do.'

'You don't,' Jake laughs. Sits beside her, takes her hands.

'Ugh. Whatever. So my mom?'

'Yes?'

'Well... She kind of thinks, um, that I've been 'sober' the last few years.'

Jake just smiles. 'So I shouldn't blow your cover?'

'Exactly.'

Mary lets the conversation end there. Stops short of what she really wants to discuss. Jake has no idea the reason for her mother's sudden visit. Maybe, Mary decides, he doesn't need to know.

***

Nights she lies awake, staring up at the ceiling. The edits slow to a trickle. Mary fills her time preparing to be an 'overseas spouse.' Downloads all the forms, forges the necessary documents. Proofs of employment, a proper lease, letters from Vanessa,

Guinevere and a few imaginary friends attesting to Jake's love and devotion. Takes care of everything, save for the appointment at the Consulate in New York and the plane tickets to get there. First, she must get through her mother and Uncle George's visit.

Books them rooms at the Britannia Hotel. Meets them at Piccadilly Station. They take the Virgin train from London on the Friday afternoon. A whirlwind visit - they're off on Sunday.

It's going to be okay, it's no big deal, Mary tells herself over and over again. And when she spots them she almost believes it.

'Mom!'

'Mary, darling. You look wonderful.'

Hugging her mother, her Uncle George. The sun is out and Mary can't wait to show them around, walks them eagerly to the hotel.

'So up there is Arndale Center, where the IRA bombed - it's all rebuilt-'

'Goodness,' her mother says. 'When was that?'

'Not that long,' says Mary.

'96,' says Uncle George. 'Father's Day, wasn't it? That's what the guidebook said. Or just before.'

'I did not know that,' says Mary. Checks in on her mother, who looks tired, pale. 'Mom, you must be jet-lagged.'

Her mother smiles. 'Maybe I'll take a quick nap. I've never been to Manchester, what a treat.'

'Wait 'till you see Didsbury where I live, and Chorlton.'

'While your mother naps I may nip out to the art museum,' says Uncle George.

'Sounds good,' says Mary. 'The play starts at eight. We can walk there from the Britannia, get a bite to eat.'

They don't see Jake until he's onstage. In the darkness of the auditorium, Mary sneaks glances at her mother, trying to gauge what she makes of him, his performance. Her mother catches her and smiles. Uncle George does too, and winks.

***

'He's amazing, isn't he?' Mary says, unable to keep still. They are in the lobby, after the show. Waiting for Jake. Mary's ducked out for a quick cigarette in front of the theater. When she rejoins her mother and Uncle George, they are deep in conversation. Body language tells her she's interrupted something.

'He was wonderful,' her mother says.

'Quite the actor,' says Uncle George. 'Your mother tells me he has a theater company, and they might be doing one of your plays soon?'

'Well.' Mary's glad Jake isn't around. 'We'll see. I need to finish the thing first.'

'Ah,' says George, and then he winks at her mother.

Mary quells her fury with a fierce smile, grateful when she sees Jake across the lobby. 'Jake!'

He spots her, then nods and grins towards her mother and Uncle George. All Mary can think is how much she adores him. His stage makeup still faint upon his face.

'Jake, hello.' Her mother gives him a hug, a kiss on the cheek.

Watching, Mary feels her head might explode. All of them together, standing there. Uncle George shaking his hand now, Jake so thin beside him.

'Shall we have a drink?' Uncle George takes over.

'Yes!'

'Sounds good,' the others echo in his wake. He's at the bar, his broad back to them.

Mary holds her breath, her mother chats with Jake. 'So nice to finally meet you,' she's saying.

'Yes, yes, likewise.'

Mary can see how his hands are shaking, the skin flushed red at the back of his neck. My baby, she thinks. It hurts to see him so vulnerable. Wants to spare him this. Keep her mother away.

Uncle George has their drinks. A Diet Coke for Mary, red wine for Jake. Her mother and George have herbal tea.

'I didn't think they made it,' says Jake, impressed.

'It's quite good,' says Mary's mother.

'What kind did you get?' asks Mary.

'Chamomile.'

'Oh right. You always drink that.'

Her mother's smile is weak. She must be tired, Mary thinks, conscious of Jake - how quickly he drinks his wine. Downs it in two gulps. His lips stained, teeth grey. He's loosened up - his voice seems loud.

'So glad you liked the play,' he's saying.

'Powerful, ending, powerful.' Uncle George is shaking his head, reminds Mary of one of the Budweiser Clydesdales, snorting and chomping at the bit.

'The ending, right? That line of Harry's kind of sums it up - *To have imagined that we could do anything decent with the world...*'

'Ah, yes. Riveting stuff.' Uncle George is riffing, out of his element.

Maybe this lasts for ten or fifteen minutes - Jake downs another two glasses of wine - Mary buys one, and Uncle George the other. The rest of them nurse their non-alcoholic drinks. Jetlag puts an end to Mary's torture. Her mother and Uncle George bow out early.

'We'll see you tomorrow night?' her mother says to Jake in parting.

Jake shoots Mary a questioning look. Then graciously, to her mother, 'I hope so. I'm going to try to make it.'

'Lovely to meet you.'

'Yes, terrific job up there. Well done,' says Uncle George.

Once they are gone, Jake and Mary join the rest of the cast at a bar on Oldham Street.

'I hear your mother's in town,' says Paul, sidling up to Mary at the bar. He's grown a moustache.

'Yup.' Mary looks for Jake. He's gone to the men's room, but he's been there awhile.

'She like the show?'

'Yea, I think she loved it.' Mary's had three large Jack and Cokes, but still, around Paul she's nervous. Gets the sense he wants Jake to himself.

'Your mom's here to meet Jake?' Paul asks, eyebrow raised. Lights a cigarette.

'Well...'

'You guys are serious.'

Mary wants to tell him they're getting married, but she hasn't had that much to drink. Keeps her mouth shut.

Later still, Mary and Jake stand on a corner near the bus station, saying goodbye. It's a Friday night, he can't sleep over.

'So tomorrow,' she says, looking up into his eyes. 'The reservation isn't until nine.'

Jake sighs, kisses her forehead. 'I'll try.'

'Jake-'

She's picked a restaurant on Beech Road, not far from the Horse & Jockey, where he'll be watching the game. Not far from his house.

'What if I'm pissed? I'll be drinking pints all afternoon.'

'Please Jake?'

'Okay.'

'No pressure.' She tries to sound nonchalant. 'We'll just have some good food, hang out. It'll be fun.'

21.

'So Mom, tonight, can we not talk about, you know, the fact Jake and I are getting married?'

'Well, I guess. It's not a secret, is it?'

'Um, well sort of.' Mary's looking around the Pret-a-Manger. She can see her Uncle George up at the counter, still ordering their coffees.

They've spent the afternoon seeing the Manchester sights. The library, the Cathedral, the Town Hall. Wandered the shops along Deansgate.

'I just, I don't want to talk about it,' Mary continues, 'not in front of Uncle George.'

'Well honey, if it makes you uncomfortable-'

'No, it's just, it's a private thing.'

'So...am I going to be involved?'

'What do you mean?'

'In your wedding. The planning, there's a lot to think about-'

'Mom! No.'

Her mother winces.

'I mean... Oh, fuck. I'm sorry. It's just... I feel like it's getting all blown out of proportion.'

Her mother's hurt turns to shock. 'Mary, we haven't even discussed it yet. Getting married is a big deal.'

'I don't want it-'

'I mean, I think I've been very good. I've been trying my hardest-' She's on the verge of tears. 'I came all the way out here-'

'Oh my God, Mom!' Mary's horrified, trying to appease her. 'I didn't mean-' Sees Uncle George on his way over. Beaming, looking so distinctly American in his Brooks Brother's suit, with his big white teeth and bowtie.

Her mother quickly pulls herself together, wipes her eyes. 'I haven't brought it up once.'

'I know Mom,' Mary whispers. 'And we can talk about it.' Gives her mother one last glance. 'Please Mom, just not tonight.'

'My lovely ladies,' Uncle George booms, setting down a tray laden with treats and steaming mugs. 'Your beverages...'

***

The afternoon drags. Mary longs to be with Jake. Alone with him, in her bed. Longs for a drink. Longs for her mother and uncle - the rest of the world - to disappear. At last it's five o'clock and Mary is seeing them off at the Britannia.

'So, Clementine at eight forty-five. You have the address?'

'Yes, yes,' says Uncle George. 'We'll take a car. See you then.'

'Mom, you going to nap?'

'I'm going to try.'

Mary watches them enter the hotel. Lingers for a moment out front, then heads for the Tesco's by the train station - for old time's sake. Buys three bottles of red wine. Even wrapped in paper bags, they clank inside her knapsack. Mary can't help but smile. Bottles to come home to. She and Jake will need them, once the dinner's over.

***

'He should be here any minute,' Mary's saying, checking her phone.

Already it's half nine. Luckily their table isn't ready. The restaurant is crowded and they are packed in at the bar.

'Cute place,' offers Uncle George. A svelte waitress in a black leotard top bumps into him so he nearly spills his wine. She doesn't apologize. The rudeness of the restaurant staff compounds Mary's torture.

It's so noisy, though, they hardly have to talk. Also, her mother's drinking red wine. Taking dainty sips - Mary doesn't miss a single one. Her glass still full, like it hasn't been touched.

'He's coming after the game, shouldn't be long.'

'Soccer?' shouts her mom.

'Here it's football,' says Uncle George. 'You know, I never thought about it, until just now - but it makes more sense.'

'What,' says Mary's mom.

'You know - like 'foot' - 'ball' - you kick it with your foot.'

'Yea,' says Mary. Bites her tongue.

Jake arrives at quarter to ten. Flushed with alcohol, but wearing a coat and tie. Mary can hardly believe it.

'Jake, you made it!' She leans up to kiss him. Even though he's had plenty to drink, he's shy. Deflects her kiss so it lands on his cheek.

'Hey Mary. Woosh, what a game.'

As he says it, Mary gets a whiff. Beneath his coat he reeks of perspiration and beer. She breathes in deep, as if to inhale the smell, keep it from her mother.

'They win?' she asks.

'Draw. But it was a great match!'

'Jake, nice to see you again,' says Uncle George, holding out his hand. Jake takes it. George slaps him on the back.

'Lovely to see you Jake,' says Mary's mother, smiling demurely. Mary can't be certain, but it seems she's almost flirting. Maybe it's the wine.

The same girl in the leotard top appears.

'Cartwright? Party of four? This way,' she says, disappearing into the dining area without bothering to see that they are following her. She leads them to their table, a rickety round top meant for a party of two or three in a stuffy back corner. Just outside the loos.

Mary has it in mind to ask if there's anything else, but one look at their surly hostess keeps her silent.

'Well, this will be cozy,' she says brightly, aware again of Jake's body odor.

Her mother and Uncle George start out open and friendly enough, and Jake is gregarious - he's nothing if not charming, Mary thinks - no matter how much he's had to drink. Anyone observing the four of them might not guess anything to be wrong. Might see a joyous gathering, clearly a young couple and perhaps a set of parents or older relatives.

'Yes, so it was a hotbed of capitalism - with the Industrial Revolution and all - you had Engels and Marx scurrying about,' Jake's explaining.

Somehow Uncle George's prompts have set him off on a brief history of Manchester. Mary, despite her anxiety, is impressed. Her mother appears to be too. Or at least, as far as Mary can tell, she's not bored or offended.

'And there was the Blitz,' Mary offers, wishing for bread. They order their food immediately, but it takes ages to arrive.

'Right,' says Jake. 'The Blitz, during the Second World War the Luftwaffe bombed the shit out of Manchester.'

Now it's Mary's turn to wince, but her mother still seems serene, if not entirely engaged.

'We went to the Cathedral this afternoon - amazing, wasn't it Mom?'

'Very impressive,' her mother agrees. 'So Jake, is your family from Manchester? Tell me about them.'

Mary holds her breath, aware her mother has just asked Jake the type of question she herself always seeks to avoid. And he responds with a wide smile, launching in on the tale of how his parents met - his father the local rugby star, his mother the prettiest girl in the village.

As he speaks, Mary wonders why she finds it so hard to ask him about his family and his past. Clearly she's told him everything there is to know about hers, albeit when she's drunk. But why hasn't she been able to ask him more about who he is? It strikes her that maybe it's not any sense he'd rather not talk about it - it's that Mary would rather not know.

'My father lives in Preston now. Runs a pub.'

'Preston? Is that far?' her mother is asking. Still hasn't made a dent in her wine.

'Forty minutes or so, by train. I see him every few months. He and my aunt come to visit, to see my son.'

I did not know that, Mary thinks.

Jake's wine glass is empty, his third, and their meal has yet to arrive.

'Here, drink mine,' Mary's mother says, sliding him her glass.

'You don't want it?' says Jake. The grey teeth and red wine moustache are back.

'No, you have it,' she says. Something in her manner, a barely detectable disdain, sets Mary on edge.

She moves closer to Jake, breathes in deep his pungent smell. Strokes his thigh under the table. I will protect you, she thinks. Hopes he can feel her love.

The food arrives. Small portions, overcooked and seasoned with a heavy hand. Nobody eats much. As for conversation, Uncle George takes over. He's a man with an inexhaustible auto-pilot for bad jokes and pedantic questions. Jake gets the full barrage:

'So you've always been interested in acting?'

'Been in anything I might know?'

'And tell me about your theater company. Why *The Revolutionaries*?'

'Mary tells me you're a published poet! What do you think of the Poet Laureate?'

'And you are able to support yourself as an actor and poet?'

'So, tell me about your son...'

At this point Mary jumps in, although Jake has been holding his own. 'Mom, you look exhausted, we should probably get the bill.'

Her mother has been sitting with an air of friendly detachment. Mary knows her mother, knows when her responses are too polite to be entirely genuine. Underneath, she is not happy. Mary wants to believe it's because she is tired, but she knows it's much more, knows exactly what it is.

***

By the time Uncle George pays the bill it's nearly midnight.

'Thank you Uncle George,' says Mary - and she means it.

'My pleasure,' he says, easing himself from the table. 'Phew, I think that jetlag has finally caught up to me. Susan?'

Mary's mother says nothing, gives him a wan smile.

The four of them exit the restaurant, stand outside on the sidewalk. At that hour Beech Road is quiet. One or two people headed home from the pub. An old man walking the dog.

Mary's called a car, and fortunately it takes no time to show up.

'So we'll see you for brunch? At the hotel?' Mary's mother asks. She seems to have shrunk. She's withered. The dinner has aged her.

'See you for brunch. We'll be there at eleven,' Mary says, hugging her. Kissing her on the cheek before she slips into the car.

'Goodnight Mrs. Cartwright!' Jake waves enthusiastically at Mary's side. They watch the car drive off with Mary's mother and Uncle George in the back. Jake turns to her. 'That was fun. You were right. Went really well, don't you think?'

'Yea.'

'Your mother's great. I really like your Uncle George too!'

***

Back at the studio, Mary wastes no time catching up to Jake. Drinks an entire bottle of wine by herself in less than twenty minutes. Starts in on the next.

Jake has crossed over. No longer up and optimistic, he's crashed hard - he's set his wine down. Lies on his back, fully clothed, on Mary's bed. He's crying.

'Jake! My God, what's the matter?'

Her acknowledgment only makes it worse. Tears stream down his face.

'Baby, oh my God.' Mary's holding him, bends down to kiss his face, wipe his tears. 'Shh, shh, it's okay. Oh honey, oh Jake.'

'It's never going to work,' he says at last. 'I'm so sorry Mary. I'm so sorry.'

'Shh, Jake, baby. Why are you apologizing? Everything is going to be fine, it's going to be great.'

'You think so?' he asks, gazing up into her eyes.

'I do. I promise.' Mary's kissing his face again. 'I'll take care of you.'

'Rescue me.'

'I will, Jake. I love you.'

'Rescue me.'

'Shh, you're the one who's rescuing me, by marrying me. I'll be safe. I'll never have to leave the country - be broke and stranded and alone! Never again. Don't you see baby? You're rescuing me!'

'Don't ever leave me. Oh God - but it can't work out - there's JJ-'

'Shh. It's going to be all right. You'll see.'

Now Mary's crying too, their tears mixed salty with their kisses.

They stay up crying, making love. Making plans and promises until nearly dawn. Close their eyes only to be bombarded by the blare of Mary's alarm clock, set for half past nine.

***

'Oh God Jake,' Mary whimpers, squeezing his hand as they enter the Britannia.

Even though she's showered, bought gum, she knows she's doomed. All that red wine. She's still drunk. The crying has puffed her eyes up.

Her mother and Uncle George are seated on a couch, surrounded by all their bags. They've already checked out.

They eat in the hotel café, just off the lobby. Mary can see her friend, the bartender Nick, at the bar. He even winks in her direction. She flinches, looks away. Sits as far away from her mother and Uncle George as possible. Hopes they can't smell the alcohol emanating from her pores. Prays they'll think it's Jake.

'So you're flying back to Boston tomorrow? From London?' Jake asks politely. He's doing his best, in the same coat and tie, now wrinkled. He's disheveled. Nibbling on a dry croissant. Mary's heart breaks, for subjecting him to the way her mother is staring.

'You must be psyched to see Truman and Ralph,' Mary butts in. Hoping to turn the conversation around by bringing up the dogs - get it going at all.

But her mother says nothing. Sits there stone-faced. Jake and Mary do what they can with Uncle George. Mary's grateful for his presence.

***

'Let's take a cab,' she says to Jake. They are standing outside the Britannia. The bus stop is just across the street and yet the thought of walking over there - sitting on board with all those people - is too much.

'Definitely,' Jake agrees. He puts an arm round her, hails a cab with the other.

They hold hands in silence the whole ride back to Mary's flat. Jake even comes up with seven pounds to pay the driver once they get there.

Inside, they strip down to their underwear. Leave the lights off, pull the shades. Bundled beneath the duvet, they cling to each other.

'Stay for awhile?' Mary says. After all, it's Sunday, he's going to have to leave.

'I want to,' he says softly. 'I'm right here.'

***

Pacing her studio that night Mary tells herself it wasn't so bad. Everything went okay. Her mother never said anything outright, did she?

Thinks back on how they parted. Her mother kissed Jake. Said how much she enjoyed meeting him.

Mary's need for her mother's validation is so great she might break in half. If she doesn't hear her mother's voice, she won't sleep. Her nerves will never be the same. Mary needs to know - needs an answer, right away.

'Mom?' She's reached her mother at her London hotel. 'You made it back okay?'

'Yes, yes, we did.'

If Mary had any doubts, what she hears in her mother's voice confirms her fears, her worst nightmare. But all she can say is, 'So, what did you think of Jake?'

'Oh honey,' her mother sighs. 'I'm so sorry. But as your mother, I have to say this. You can't marry him.'

'What?'

'Mary, I'm sorry. The way he drank at dinner-'

'Oh my God. How dare you!'

'Mary, you don't know anything about him. Honey, he has that little boy-'

'Mom-'

'Please Mary, what's the rush? Why not date each other for a year?'

'We're in love, we just want to be together - if I leave we could be apart for months-'

'Mary, plenty of people have long distance-'

'You don't understand.'

'Honey, you can't do this, you just can't.'

'Why not?'

'Oh Mary.'

'You know what? I can't talk about this. I have to go now.'

Even as she says it, Mary feels like she's ten years old.

'I'm sorry, mom.'

'Mary, honey-'

Mary hangs up the phone. Resumes pacing the studio, trembling, weighted with shame.

Breathe, she tells herself, breathe. Pours a glass of wine. Lights a cigarette. Reminds herself she's not alone. Everything will work out. She still has faith.

22.

In the days that follow, her mother calls. Mary doesn't pick up. Uncle George does his part, but Mary ignores him as well. Deletes their emails. Looks both ways when she steps out her door, half expecting them to leap from the bushes and accost her.

The fallout with her mother sees her shift into high gear, gives her fresh courage when it comes to ironing out the marriage details with Jake.

'Here's the deal. I need to get a fiancé visa. I have to fly to New York. What's your passport number? Your mother's maiden name? Your father's occupation?'

'You need all this information-?' Jake is saying nervously. 'What are they going to do with it?'

'Nothing, don't worry,' Mary snaps. 'I've already forged most of the documents anyway.'

'You have?' Jake is aghast. 'Like what?'

'Oh, you know. Proof you can support me, a lease for where we are going to live, letters from our friends saying how we met, how long they've known us. Stuff like that.'

Jake has gone pale.

'Don't worry,' Mary sighs. 'It's just going to be stashed away in a file somewhere. Nobody's ever going to see.'

'Okay,' Jake says. 'Maybe it's better if I don't know.'

'Yea, except I may need your passport. Is it okay if I take it with me?'

'Ah, sure. I guess.'

***

With most of her savings, Mary books a flight to New York, pays the fee for the visa.

'Stay alive. I will come back for you,' she says when she sees Jake the night before she leaves, mimicking Daniel Day Lewis in *The Last of the Mohicans*.

'Baby, I wish there was more I could do-'

'Don't worry,' Mary says, placing a finger on his lips before he can respond. 'No matter how long it takes, no matter how far. I will find you.'

Deep down neither one of them is really sure she's going to pull it off. There's no margin for error. She's booked her flights so she has just under ten hours on the ground in New York City to do what she needs to do.

She goes straight to the British Consulate from the airport. Her appointment is at three in the afternoon. When her number is called, a friendly, balding Englishman riffles through her paperwork, asks her a few questions.

'Passports?'

'Here you go.'

'And do you have any plans for the wedding?'

'Yes sir, we want to do it at City Hall. More romantic.'

The man raises his spectacles and looks at her, then winks.

'I know what you mean. Wish my daughter thought like you. She wanted a big 'do. Three hundred people she invited.'

'Yowza,' says Mary.

'Okay, then, just have a seat. They'll call you when your passport is ready.'

Mary has several moments of concern, when people who went after her are handed their passports with the shiny new visas. But just before the Consulate is to close, at quarter to six, Mary is called to the window.

'Here you go miss,' says another man, this one younger.

'Thank you,' says Mary, the excitement rising inside her. 'Thank you so much.'

By half eight she's back at JFK. Her flight leaves at ten.

Baby, we did it! On my way. Xo

On the plane, she confides in the stewardess, 'I just got my fiancé visa! I'm getting married!' Even though she's not in first class they give her a champagne miniature.

When she lands in the UK she passes through Immigration with ease. In the cab on her way back to Didsbury, Mary is amazed looking out the window. It's not just the sun is shining - everything seems to have come into bloom in the twenty-four hours she's been gone. It's like Paradise.

23.

'I don't understand - what do you mean you can't come over?'

It's Saturday evening, nearly eleven o'clock. Mary's been waiting for Jake since six. The Indian takeaway she ordered hours ago is still unopened, gone cold on the counter. It's two Saturdays in a row now that Jake has been a no-show. Mary is more than suspicious - she's starting to panic.

They are set to wed in less than a week. Mary has used the last of her money to rent her studio another month. The plan is they will be married, and Jake will divide his time between the two households. At least until he can break the news to his ex he's going to move in with Mary.

'I don't understand why you don't just tell her now,' Mary says.

'It's just, it's complicated. Remember I told you she has this other boyfriend? Well, they broke up.'

'So... I don't understand-?'

'She's having a rough time. I think if I told her I was moving right now, it would freak her out.'

'Baby, this conversation is freaking me out!'

'Shh, shh. I know, I know. I just don't want to make things too calamitous for JJ.'

'Oh, right.' Mary is silenced. She's not going to argue with him when it comes to the little boy. Won't be the one to come between a child and his father.

'That's cool, baby. I understand,' she says at the time.

Now, a few short weeks later, something smells horribly wrong.

'Jake, this is crazy. What's going on?'

'Mary, I'm sorry. You have to bear with me - hang on - I have to get off the phone-'

'WHAT?!' Jake clicks off and Mary stands there. 'Oh my God.'

Jake's calls begin at nine the following morning.

Mary doesn't pick up, doesn't check her messages or read his texts. Doesn't move from the couch, where she tries to read the Jean Rhys biography, the television on low volume in the background.

Her phone has stopped ringing and it's coming up on three in the afternoon when she hears footsteps in the drive. Pebbles pinging against the window.

'Mary!'

Hears Jake's voice calling out, urgent but low. So nobody else in the building - in the neighborhood - will hear.

Mary remains on the couch, puts her book down.

More pebbles at the window. 'Mary, please, I have to talk to you.'

When she finally goes to the door, he's in a state. Pale, hollow-eyed, says not a word. Takes her in his arms like he's just come back from a war. In his leather jacket, he grips her hard. At first she wants to pull away, but he's shaking. Desperate in a way she's never seen before.

'Shh, baby.' Now she's the one stroking him. The tables have turned.

***

They break out a bottle of red wine. Jake won't stop pacing. Puffy bloodshot eyes. He's been crying.

'Jake, what's the matter? You're scaring me.'

'Mary, I'm sorry, I don't know. I don't know what to do.'

'What's going on?'

'Okay.' Jake stops pacing, he's facing her. Lips trembling.

'Jake-'

He looks down, then off to the side. Starts talking. 'I think maybe it was the success of the play - or - I don't know…'

'What?'

'My ex wants to get back together with me.'

'Oh. But, you don't want to - or do you?'

'No - God no!' And Jake is upon her, hugging her again, holding on to her dearly.

'Jake, shh, it's ok.'

He pulls away. Takes a breath. Spots his wine and downs it. 'The thing is, she's pissed about us-'

'But, I mean, she's known about me all along?'

'Yes. I don't know though. She flipped out on me last night. Said unless I end it with you, she's going to move away. I'll never see JJ.' Tears have filled his eyes, he's close to sobbing.

'Shh, Jake, it's ok. She can't do that.'

'She can, she's going to-'

'Jake, it's going to be ok. We'll get through this.'

'Mary - I just think maybe we should wait-'

'Wait?'

'Yea.'

'Like, not get married?'

'Yea.'

The room has turned into a hellish mélange of bright lights and too much glass. Mary backs up towards her bed, has to lean against it.

'And maybe...' Jake's still talking, inside Mary's begging him to stop, for just a minute. 'If we could not see each other - just for a little while - until things settle down.'

'You're dumping me.'

'I'm not. Mary please.' Tears are streaming down his face now. 'I'm asking you to wait.'

'Oh my God.' Mary's crying too.

'I told her - I told her we broke up.'

'Oh Jake.'

'Baby no - it's just - the timing's not right. Will you wait for me?' He's sobbing now, reaches out to her.

She wants to shake him off, wants to punch him. But she stands there, staring at their hands, all blurred.

'Just go-'

'Mary?'

'Jake, please. I'll be okay. Just go. I need to be alone.' Jake tries once or twice to touch her, but Mary's turned away. 'Get out Jake.'

And so he goes.

In a trance, Mary moves from where she's standing by the bed, to the kitchen. Takes down another bottle of wine. Moves from kitchen to couch, from couch to window, window to bedside. In silence. Back to the kitchen, for more wine.

Can't bear the thought of calling anyone. Just wants to disappear. Turns out the lights. Curls up tight under the covers, glad for the muffled void.

***

At first she thinks it's her dream. Cracks like thunder. Rattling. Then she's conscious. Someone at her window. Jake.

Still half asleep, she lets him in. He's upon her. Bloodied.

'Jesus, what happened? You get in a fight?'

He's cut above his eyebrow. Incoherent. 'Mary, Mary-'

'Jake, there now.' She turns on the light and he winces. Takes off his jacket, staggers into her.

'You're drunk,' she says. 'Sit down.'

'She threw me out.'

'Who did?'

'Sara.'

Hits her like a plank. Her name, the ex.

'Mary, can I stay with you?'

'Jake. I don't-'

'Please Mary-'

'Jake.'

'I want to be with you.'

Mary sighs, sits down beside him. Strokes his head. Gets up again.

'Where are you going?'

'Shh. It's okay. Just turning out the light.'

'Could you get me a glass of water?'

'Sure.' Mary goes to the sink, turns on the faucet. Holds her hands under the cold water and lets it flow. Fills a glass and switches off the tap. Gets the lights.

Jake has stripped to his boxers, waits in her bed.

'Jake? Jake, here's some water.'

He sits up. 'Thanks.' Drains the glass and hands it back, wraps his arms around her.

She's searching for the words. 'Jake?'

'Yes?'

'I need to ask you something.'

Jake is silent, but she can tell by his breathing, he's waiting.

'This whole time, you and Sara...' Mary hesitates. Saying her name, like holding a bullet in her mouth. 'Where do you sleep Jake?'

The pause is what she'd dreaded.

'Jake?'

'Well, most of the time she's never there - she's always at her boyfriend's.'

'Jake, do you have your own room, or do you and Sara share a bed?'

'I mean, half the time I wind up sleeping in JJ's room-'

'Jake. You share a bed.'

'It's not like that.'

Mary wriggles out of his embrace. Gets up from the bed and finds her cigarettes.

'Mary-'

'No Jake. She's not really your ex, is she? You guys have been together this whole time. That's why she beat you up tonight, isn't it? She threw you out. Oh my God. I think I'm going to be sick.'

'Mary no, I love you.'

'Jake don't.'

But he's up and at her side, pleading. 'Mary, I want to be with you.'

'I don't believe you. You lied.'

'I didn't - I just left some things out.'

'That's the same as lying.'

'I don't want to lose JJ! Mary, its been over between us for years - she had another boyfriend!'

'So now you have a girlfriend, and that's not okay with her?'

'Yes! She calls the shots, we're not married, if she decides she wants to take JJ, not let me see him, the law is on her side.'

'Jake... I don't know.' But Mary is softening.

The conversation goes on like this. Maybe Mary gets tired. In spite of everything, her love for Jake is still strong. And now the element of competition. Mary's not ready to let go. To walk away, when she's invested everything. The thought is unbearable.

But before she lets him back in her bed she makes him promise.

'You'll never leave me?'

'Never.'

'The two of us, against the world?'

'Mary, yes.'

'You'll always be my home?'

'I'll always be your home. I want to marry you. I promise. I'll stay with you forever. I love you.'

'Okay. You can stay.'

***

That night he holds nothing back. Takes her with a fury that makes her feel used. It's the first time he comes inside her.

Afterwards, lying there in the dark, she sees clear. That up until now, he's been cheating.

***

They wake to Jake's phone on the chair by the bed, vibrating. He gets up, scrolls through the messages. Sucks in his breath, goes pale.

'What is it baby?'

'My things are in garbage bags out in the street.'

'Fuck. Okay, we'll go get them.'

Jake has his trousers on, locates his shoes, his shirt. 'No, it's okay. We probably shouldn't be seen together. I'll go. You wait here.'

'You need some money?' Mary offers, and Jake hesitates. 'Why don't you take a car. You'll never be able to carry everything.'

'You're right,' he says. 'Good idea.'

'Here.' She jumps from the bed, finds her wallet. Gives him everything she has.

'I might be awhile,' he says before he goes.

'I know,' says Mary. 'Do what you have to do.'

He leaves without kissing her goodbye. But what's worse is the smell that hangs in the air when he's gone.

24.

The next forty-eight hours, Jake takes to Mary's bed. He barely moves. Turns off his phone against the onslaught of texts.

'I'm never going to see JJ again!'

'Shh, you are. She can't do that.'

'She can. I've let him down. He must be so confused.'

'It's going to be okay.'

'It's not. It won't be the same.'

Mary is beside herself. In two days they are getting married. She tries everything - food, he won't eat - drink, he just gets drunk, starts to cry and passes out - sex, he's distant, they don't connect.

She goes shopping. Buys a new duvet cover, dishwashing liquid. The crumpets Jake likes, lamb sausages.

On the way home, she gets caught in the rain. Stands under the awning of a ninety-nine pence store, waiting for the torrent to subside. Watches the water cascading off the cars parked at the curb. Mary is mesmerized, thinks of Guinevere and Vanessa. She hasn't spoken to either of them in weeks. They don't know about her wedding date. Maybe she's afraid to jinx it. 'We'll grab our witness off the street,' she tells Jake, hoping it will make him smile.

And her mother. It's only been a few weeks since she was in Manchester. Her last email arrived five days ago, but Mary deleted it, unread.

'I think I need to take something,' Jake says when she returns home.

'How about some Advil?'

'Ok.' She can tell it's not what he had in mind. 'Do we have any red wine?'

At least he has the guts to ask. It's barely half four, but the sky has cleared. 'I'll run out for some - hang tight.'

Jake doesn't move. Offers no cash. All the money that's being spent is hers. He wants her to rescue to him, and she's doing her best.

Before she's out the door she thinks of something. 'You know what? This might help you baby.' Wades through the rubble of garbage bags cluttering the hallway - all his worldly possessions. Pulls a disk from a stack on the counter and sets up her CD player on the floor beside the bed.

'Here, let me just get these things on you,' she says, untangling her earphones. His eyes are closed even though he's awake. He won't look at her. Face covered with stubble and puffier than normal.

Staring down at him, she experiences a flash of rage. Primal, unexpected - it throws her off balance. But it's there and gone. Leaves a tenderness in its wake that draws her to him. She kisses him on the cheek, breathes him in. Waits for him to kiss her back and he does. Slides his hand down her side, then slips it in the waist of her pants.

His eyes are open and it's a faint one - sad even - but he's smiling.

Afterwards, they are lying on their backs. He's stroking her hand. 'You want to go get that wine?'

'Oh shit, yea. Sorry.' She puts on her pants, sees the CD player. 'Hang on, you need to listen to this.' Sticks the headphones back on him.

'What is it?'

'My self-hypnosis CD. To help you relax.'

'Does it work?'

'Shh. Just close your eyes and breathe. I'll be back with the wine.'

Now it's five o'clock so she feels better about him drinking. Buys two bottles of Merlot at the seedy Cooperative. It's cheaper there, not that the extra two pounds makes a difference. Her savings are gone. She's now well into her overdraft.

When she returns they sit on the couch in front of the TV, drinking the red wine and watching *Big Brother*.

'I can't stand those twins,' Mary says at one point.

'I kind of like Chantelle,' Jake says. 'She's hot.'

In the morning, Mary makes a suggestion. The situation is more than she alone can fix.

'Why don't you go see one of your guy friends? Just, you know, you need support. You're a great guy, people like you. It might be good to get out of the house.'

'Yea?' Jake looks up from his croissant, bought fresh that morning. She's doing everything in her power to keep him comfortable.

'Yea. Meet someone for lunch,' she says. 'Baby, life goes on. It's going to work out.'

'Yeah, maybe I will. I'll see what Paul is up to.'

Mary expects this, and even though he's not her top choice, she tells herself, Paul's an adult, someone who knows Jake. A trusted friend. Someone who can help him through this.

Already Jake is brighter. Makes a date with Paul. Takes a shower. Even kisses her goodbye on the cheek before he goes.

***

Mary doesn't start to worry until eight o'clock, when he's still not back. Calls his cell phone and leaves a message when he doesn't pick up.

'Jake, just wondering where you are. Hope it went well. Sure you're feeling better, guess maybe you're out with the boys? Don't forget, tomorrow is our big day, hehe. City Hall at eleven - hey, if you're with Paul, see if he wants to be our witness! Anyway. Baby, call me, just so I know you're okay...'

Sends a text.

Baby, you okay? where are you? come home:-) xxx

Nothing. Goes to buy cigarettes and a few bottles of wine.

Watches *Big Brother*, watches the news, finishes the first bottle, calls Jake eight more times. Leaves two more messages.

'Baby, I'm starting to get a little worried. Where are you? Please, please call me- please come home. It's our last night! Tomorrow we have to be at City Hall by eleven...'

'Jake, call me please. I don't understand. I love you, where are you? Come home...'

Sends another text.

Jake, where are you? please at least just text me you're okay I love you xxx

Tells herself maybe he lost his phone, maybe he's out with the boys, having a stag. It could be nothing. Well into the second bottle. Goes from concern to anger to despair.

Feels it in the silence. He's not coming back.

Looks Paul up in the phone book. Amazed it never occurred to her earlier. It's so easy. Finds his number, his address. It's nearing midnight, two bottles of wine on an empty stomach - so calling anyone is probably a bad idea. But she's desperate.

'Hello?'

'Paul, it's Mary-'

'Hello Mary. Jake is here.'

She's leaning on the counter, has the spins. 'Oh phew!' she gushes. The words tumble out fast, 'Can I talk to him - please - he get my messages? I don't understan-'

'Mary, calm down. He can't come to the phone right now.'

'What? I don't understand - please Paul, can I talk to him?'

'Not now Mary.'

'I don't get it - why couldn't he call me - I was so worried - so scared!'

'He's had a bad night. He's not well. Let's leave it at that.'

'Please Paul-' Nausea rising to her throat.

'Mary-'

'Why? Just let me talk him-' She's crying, sinking down, 'Please Paul-'

'Go to bed, Mary-'

'Paul, no-'

'Mary, I'm going to hang up now.'

The line goes dead. In her mind she's thinking she will take a cab to Paul's address, storm the place, anything to get to Jake.

First, she just needs to lie down for a sec.

***

Wakes up on the floor. Sees the numbers on her crap DVD player from Woolworth's flashing, 11:13, 11:13, 11:13… Mary is a believer in signs from the universe, and this one is bad. If 11:11 is for wishing, 11:13 is all your wishes be damned.

Even so, Mary keeps staring at the clock. Her head pounds, is full of lead. She just needs to stay right where she is for a bit.

Hears the faint sounds of traffic. Outside, the birds have long been chirping. The sun is bright. Now it's 11:26. And then it strikes her like a flaming spear in the gut-

Today she was supposed to get married. 'Oh my God, Jake!'

Rolls over onto her stomach. Presses her face into the floor. Stares intimately at the rug fibers, filthy microscopic pipe cleaners littered with cigarette ash and dribbles of red wine.

Sits up, rubs her head. Now she wants to cry - but it's fleeting. A crumpled pack of cigarettes tempts her from the floor. There's three left.

Lights up. Inhaling the first drag, she feels better. Now she needs a drink.

It's 11:34. Maybe there's wine left over from last night.

Thumps over to the kitchen. Her thighs are bare and moving makes the place behind her knees that was starting to sweat feel cool again. Finds two empty bottles. A third, half full, teeters at the edge of the sink. Uncorked, fermenting in the sunlight.

Instead of pouring the wine out, she drinks. Everything inside her roils up hot and suffocating - she might throw up. Still, she downs a good portion of it. Pauses, takes a few drags on her cigarette.

'Damn.' Says it out loud, like she's talking to her dog - except she doesn't have one. Finishes the rest of the wine and knows she's going to go out and buy more - and more cigarettes. But first she needs to sit down on the couch for a little.

The numbers on the DVD player are now flashing 12:36. All Mary can think of is somehow she managed to miss 12:34.

She hasn't moved. Cigarette ashes at her feet. And there's her cell phone, still silent - no word from Jake.

Thinks on the day she went to Primark in City Centre - was it only a few weeks ago? To pick out a wedding dress. That day nothing could touch her. She was nearly home free. Loved the idea of being married in a dress that only cost five pounds.

It would have been a good thing, she tells herself - or tries to, except the thought is interrupted by a wail from deep inside that propels her from the couch towards the bed. The CD player with the earphones still attached is right where she left it.

'Oh Jake.'

The navy blue chinos she wears every day, with the heart patches sewn across the knee, are halfway beneath the dresser. Where they landed when Jake tore them off her. Was it less than 24 hours before?

Mary puts them on, and a tattered bra. Still wearing the t-shirt she slept in, the same one she wore the day before. Finds ten pounds and change in the pants pockets. Enough for cigarettes and wine.

Walking to the store, she misses her sunglasses. Jake has them, loves her American Ray Bans. Wears them even at night in the pub, like a kid.

Dares think about where he might be. In the sunshine, walking down the Wilmslow Road, on his way home? More likely sitting in a pub, with a pint, sunglasses on. Or at Paul's - in bed, head stashed beneath the pillows, prone. Just like he was in her studio the last few days.

At the Cooperative now, wandering the isles. Wilted veggies in bins to one side, generic brand dairy products to the right. If she cared to glance at the labels on any of these items, she'd be willing to bet money they were past their due date. Why she's even in this aisle she's not sure. Countless times she's been there, knows the layout. The alcohol is in the far aisle, on the opposite side of the store.

Maybe it's just there's something comforting about being there at all. As if it's any normal Tuesday afternoon, and she's just popped out for what she needs later, for supper. Sure, a bottle of wine - but maybe some milk, a few cans of beans, cheese, or pasta?

Only now she's in the liquor aisle. Surrounded by cheap wine. There's no denying, it feels so criminal and yet so right. Three bottles for a fiver - today's her lucky day. That means a twenty-pack of cigarettes as well.

'Now you're set for the rest of the afternoon,' the kid at the till says, and even though she's buzzed she's still flabbergasted. How the fuck does he know?

Takes her change as soberly as she can, but even as the bottles clink in the plastic carrier bag, she knows it's futile.

They both know what she's destined for on that idyllic, dazzling spring day.

hey mary- jake's not doing so well. he's going to stay with me- is it ok if I stop by in a bit to pick up some of his things? paul

Mary is back on the couch. An empty bottle of wine at her feet. Cradles another, she's sitting up. Barely. Swaying, eyes unfocused. TV on in the background. An infomercial about some elderly retirement community in Wales. A man with white mutton chops is smiling and saying in an accent she struggles to understand, 'Trust your loved ones to Cameo Acres. Modeled after the Swedes. A Utopian community in the foothills.'

Mary starts with a jolt. Was she dreaming? Looks at the TV - it's not on. Her cigarette burned down to the filter.

Footsteps in the drive - she's not dreaming anymore. She's wide-awake, heart pounding in her chest.

Keys jangling - she knows it's Paul but she can't bear to see him. Sprints to the bathroom, locks the door behind her. Leans against it - she might be sick.

Then silence. Only her panting. The bathroom window just behind the toilet is open and Mary can see trees, what's left of a sunshine-y day, now waning. No clouds. Sky as blue as a tropical sea but it's no longer gentle, it's thick and overripe. And Mary's thinking, up there is heaven, God, what I would give to be there.

'Mary!' Paul cries out from a distance.

She's had so much to drink she might be under water. Totters towards the pile of her clothes under the sink - jeans, her favorite sweatshirt, her Converse. Despite wine-logged limbs she slips into the jeans. Then with the sweatshirt, over her head.

'Mary!'

Mary's moving fast now. Shaky, starting to sweat. Feet half in her sneakers she stumbles, one knee on the toilet, then the other, now her head is through the window, now she's tumbling onto the gravel of the back drive.

A woman walking past, baby in pram, ogles her, accusing. Eyes say, 'What the fuck are you doing?' Mary sees her, quickly looks down. She's crouched like a runner, the veins on her hands engorged, her body throbbing with alcohol. Jams her feet all the way into her shoes, does the laces. It's an effort, but somehow she makes it up and running. Hits the sidewalk, flat-footed and loud. Wheezing, panting, soles whacking dull on the pavement. But there's a slight breeze, it catches her in the face and her eyes shut against the sun. She's running now, running in a sprint, not thinking, going nowhere, just running, running away from there.

Later. She's in the village, trying to seem normal - hand braced on a storefront, trying to stand upright. Sweat soaked through but the afternoon is changing to evening, the air cooling, she just needs to keep moving.

A corner shop. Reeks of stale smoke and incense. Brown-skinned man at the counter half-hidden behind a racing form. Porno magazines blocked by construction paper. Rothman's and Dutch Master's.

'Help ye?' asks the store clerk, and Mary meets his eyes a second. Hands in her pockets - finds nothing. She has no cash. Gum, mints, another pack of cigarettes - all of it's off-limits.

Tesco's. Mistake to come here. Searing lights, so many aisles - and they are endless. It's like OZ. Alien and overstuffed. In the bakery section she nicks a roll. Ripping out great hunks - the soft part in the middle. Stuffing it in her mouth. Trying to eat quickly so she's not caught stealing. Trying to swallow. Panicking. Racing to the exit, to the parking lot behind the building, where she bends over. Lets rip. Coughing, saliva, wadded dough spewing everywhere. Tears streaming down her face, but she can breathe again.

Over by the bus stop. Stands under the shelter like it's raining, like she's waiting for a bus. Alone, the sky now a heartbreaking shade of purple. The bus pulls up and she climbs on, without thinking about it, like she has somewhere to go. The driver's on his cell phone - he doesn't stop her for not paying the fare - only nods.

Mary lurches towards the back, thinking she would have liked to kiss his face if not for the plexiglass between them. She goes right to the very end, on the lower level - the most naff spot on the bus - but it's her favorite. Slides all the way in, so she can lean her head against the window.

Down the Wilmslow Road, past all the ancient trees, the blooming shrubbery, past all the pretty stone houses. Corner stores, liquor stores - lots and lots of liquor stores.

Mary's rubbing her hands on her jeans at the knees. Her head hurts. Her heart hurts, she wants to lean over, pass right through the wall of the bus, and fall onto the cement. Imagines herself tumbling down, rolling over and over and over, wearing down, crumbling to bits, scattering everywhere, disappearing into nothing.

Instead she bangs her head against the window and a black girl across the aisle looks over at her and then quickly looks away.

The City Centre. Stepping out amidst the trams and so many people Mary has to resist the urge to drop to the sidewalk right then and there and curl up, eyes buried in the crook of her elbow, fists pressed into her ears. To take cover from the world. Sees herself frozen on the ground like someone unearthed at Pompeii.

Like a sleepwalker she passes through the revolving doors of the Britannia Hotel. Crosses the lobby and enters the bar. Nick the bartender is right there where he was the last time she saw him and she thinks she might cry. She's so happy to see a familiar face. He gives her the same nod he always does - like it's no big deal, like she comes in all the time. Like they're friends. And if he sees she's drunk he doesn't let on. Besides, she thinks, when has she ever not been drunk when he's seen her?

'Hey-yo.' She's pleased as punch. She's not gonna cry.

'Hey New York. Back for more research?' he smiles. 'What'll it be?'

She can't quite remember. So she shrugs, shakes her head, looks down. Her eyelids betray her. They're twitching out of control.

'Red wine? Merlot?' Nick says, helping her out.

She wants to say 'That would be perfect' but all she comes up with is 'Thath.' Now it's time to cough or get the hell out. Nick looks away - he knows better.

Mary sits, drinks the glass of water that's materialized at her elbow. The whole room is spinning slowly, everyone inside it moving like wispy dancers. Mary notices she can't feel her nose or her mouth.

At the far end of the bar, Nick is corking a bottle for a stout couple. The woman has Farrah hair, large teeth. She's laughing. The man leans over the bar, he's grinning. Gold teeth and a Rolex watch. When he flicks a cigarette from his pack of Kools down the bar at Mary, she thinks, cool. Also, she doesn't remember asking him for one.

The chandelier glitters at center of the ceiling. Blowsy drapes. The bar is nearly full up. Outside it is night. Brass fixtures gleam with Mary's reflection - only upside down and warped - like circus mirrors. Ebony paneling on the bar and someone has bought her a glass of red wine. More large men crowd the TV in the far corner, all in light blue jerseys, Manchester City fans. The wine in her glass is so dark it might be blood. Mary has to get up. Before she falls off her stool.

Looking down, crossing the ugly tortoise-patterned carpet. Keep going. Pushing through the glass doors at the rear of the bar. Moving on legs like poorly-attached stilts. Down an endless mirrored hallway. Staring back her, multiplied, a ghastly grinning girl. Her lips too red, and smeared. She's a hyena, back from the kill. Hair on end.

The ladies room door is heavy and green and Mary pushes through it like she's won. Straight to the loo in the farthest corner where she bolts the door and sits, safe, hidden, in blissful silence.

Wakes with a jerk. Voices, giggling just beyond the doors. Where is she? Green walls, she's still sitting on the toilet. Her limbs so heavy, just to sit it feels good. Sound of the tap running, a distant flush. Voices echoing gently off the walls. This hollow cavern, she thinks, nice white noise - a generator somewhere -

keeping this hotel moving along. The dear Britannia. The kind Britannia. Her friend.

Head pressed against the cool side wall. She must get up. Get out. Is able to stand. Flushes, even though she was sitting on the lid the whole time. The ladies room is empty now. It's hers. Runs the tap and splashes water on her face. Could stay there for hours. Only she hears more footsteps in the hall, laughter. Quickly she dries her face and hands and as the door swings open - more blondes in flashy dresses - Mary slips out.

On Portland Street the sidewalks are packed - what she sees is a kaleidoscope of neon, flashing lights, bare flesh, whites of eyes and teeth and so many cars, bearing down heavy and fast. It's too much. She hasn't escaped the urge to sink down onto the sidewalk. But she can't, she has to move on. She needs to get away from all these people, she needs a place to sit. Her wish is to be near the ocean - on a beach - to sit on the sand and just stare at the waves.

She trips, slams into a large man - something hard, bone - smashes into her jaw-

'Oi! Watch it!' he snarls.

She feels the others in his group staring, taking her in. Tastes the blood on the inside of her cheek. But she keeps going, she doesn't look back. Hair in her face, she's running now, up through Chinatown. Inside she's crying, sobbing. *Just get me away from here. Get me someplace silent, someplace calm. Oh please God get me away from here.* She's running blindly. Looking only at the ground. The city receding, sounds muffled by the pounding of her own heart.

Stumbling along the path by the canals. It's gone pitch black and windy, like it might start pissing down. She's zipped all the way up in her sweatshirt but still she's shivering. Aching - her calves hurt, the bones in her feet - she must stop. Takes a seat on a rusted bench, there's no one else around. Laughter, traffic, sirens and shouts in the distance. The city can have it, she thinks. She's fine. Puts her thumb in her mouth. *This is nice.* The water so still, rippled, inviting.

***

Opens her eyes with a start. *Where am I? How long was I sleeping?*

There's kids, sounds of thumping, angry shouts. A group of them at the edge of the canal, less than twenty yards away. Gathered around something. Nobody looking in her direction. She's numb, not sure how long she's been sitting there.

'Kill it!' the kids are shouting.

As her eyes grow accustomed to the dark, she sees the bats and sticks they're wielding. Smashing at something on the ground, again and again. Whatever it is, it's trapped, pinned. From the tone of their blows she can tell it's something living they're trying to kill. Her heart stops and she's paralyzed, her senses primed - she sees clearly now - it's a dog.

'Harder! Hit the head.'

The group is five or seven strong. She sees their bikes nearby.

'Smash it! Here - let me! C'mon!'

They are beating the dog mechanically now - it hasn't moved. She goes to cry out but no sound comes. She tries to stand. Now they've stopped.

'Go on! Grab the fekkin' tail - 'urry up'

Another one kicks, another lands a vicious blow to the dog's skull. And then she hears it - the dog yelps. It's faint but dragged out - a shriek of pain, a death shriek - twisting Mary's insides. She's up from the bench, her throat closed up almost completely but still she's on her feet - like in a dream where she can't move fast enough, can barely move at all.

'Mo - mmmo - mmmother FUCKersssssssss - Aaaaaaaaaaaaaa -'

The kids look up, startled. The one holding the dog's hind end drops it, then scrambles to grab hold of it again. Mary's nearly on them - now they're scurrying, struggling with their quarry to the edge of the canal. She's moving faster now. They're swinging the dog - over land, over water - taunting her - laughing, sneering.

'Aaaaaaaah!'

She's barely a yard away - so close she's almost - she's sliding, out of control - slamming into the group of them. There's a splash and she knows it's the dog. Now she's on the ground, they're kicking her - another strikes her head with something hard - a rock.

The little bastard! She springs back to her feet - blind, her head wet, hot - she's clawing, kicking, tearing with all she's got - then someone head-butts her in the gut.

Wind knocked out - she's falling backwards. Suspended in air. Sounds of shouting, a great scuffle behind her.

'Hurry! Get the fuck out, mate!'

'She's gone in the canal!'

Plunging into the black water.

First basso glugging all around her, then silence. It's shocking how heavy her clothes have become. Even with the adrenaline kicking in, her limbs are leaden and hard to move. Starts to struggle and then stops. It feels divine.

Closes her eyes and lets go.

Her body sinks.

26.

Something knocks her in the face. Pain shatters her jaw, bringing her back to consciousness. Eyes opened wide in the darkness, panic. *I want to breathe. I want to live!* Thrashing in her heavy clothes. She slips the sweatshirt off. Now she's rising, rising towards the lights, towards the surface. Through the water she can see the moon.

Head bursting into the cold air, she's gasping, wheezing, bawling, choking, spitting up water. Something is splashing beside her - the dog. She reaches for it, lunging in mad strokes to the edge of the canal, to the wall. The dog goes limp, it's passed out.

'What the fuck?' says a man's voice - heavy footsteps, he's running now, running towards her.

'Jesus, someone's in there?' says another.

'You there?' the first calls out - he's at the edge, but several yards down.

'Help!' Mary struggles for a hold on the wall of granite rocks. 'Help!' she says again. Sobbing outright, shaking, still holding the dog, trying to keep its head above water.

'Jesus! You all right?'

'Holy fuck - hang on.'

There are two of them. Large, strapping men. Mary sees them as shadows, their voices filling her with comfort, with hope.

'Hang on! We'll get you out.'

Now one is on the ground, reaching down towards her, the second man behind him, holding his legs. 'Here, grab my arms, I'll pull you up.'

'The dog,' Mary says.

'Wot? PJ! She's got a fucking dog in here!'

'Please-' says Mary. 'It won't hurt you.'

'No, no, it's okay,' he says. 'I like dogs - just didn't expect it. You going to be able to hang on?'

'I'm good,' says Mary. Even manages a weak smile.

'Okay PJ - I have the dog - sit tight on me legs, yeah?'

Carefully the men lift the dog out - it's a Staffordshire, a small one - perhaps a puppy or maybe just a runt. No more than thirty pounds.

'Hey, there you go. Jesus, somebody did a number on this dog.'

'Is it okay?' Mary calls out. The thought that the dog might not live has her seized with fresh panic.

'Still breathing, luv,' one of the men says. 'Let's get you out.'

The first man is now before her, reaching out his hands and she takes them - they are so warm. Inching her way up to his shoulders, he has her around the waist now. She can feel his whiskers against her cheek. Conscious of getting him all wet. He doesn't seem to notice, he's intent on lifting her. Slowly, by inches, he moves backwards, pulling her up, pulling her out. Water streaming from her clothes, great gallons of water, as she's dragged over the edge and onto the ground. Lying there panting, sobbing and laughing.

'Th-thank you, thank you-'

'Jesus Christ!' the one who stayed above says, lighting a cigarette. He's the bigger of the two - and both of them are large, dressed in jeans, work boots, bomber jackets.

The one who pulled her out is taking his jacket off, wrapping it round her shoulders. 'Here take this. It's bloody cold - you wouldn't think it was almost summer, right?'

Mary nods, she's stroking the dog. It's curled up, shivering now, so she knows it's alive.

'You want an ambulance, yeah?' says the one who's smoking, pacing.

'Huh?'

'You have a right gash - you don't feel it? What happened? You took a tumble?'

The other is rubbing her outside the jacket, warming her up. 'You're going to be okay? What happened?'

'These kids-' is all she can manage.

'Fuck.'

'Yeah. Seen 'em down here. Up to no good.'

'I, I um... They were gonna kill the dog.'

'Fukkin-A,' says one of the guys, shaking his head.

There is an awkward silence, then, 'Bet this isn't how you planned to be spending your Tuesday night.'

'Nope,' says Mary, a small grin creeping up on her face.

The guy who's pacing kneels down to check the dog. 'Mates, she's bleeding pretty bad.'

'Oh no!'

'Best get her to a vet,' says the kind one at her side. 'C'mon, we'll take you.'

The walk to the road where they catch a cab isn't far, but Mary makes her way unsteady, stares at the ground. The dog leaks a trail of blood.

'I'm Randy by the way,' says the one who has given her his coat. He says his name like 'Ran-duh.' 'This this is my mate PJ.' He nods to his friend who walks just ahead of them, carrying the dog.

'Mary,' she says.

'American?' asks Randy.

'Yup.'

PJ shoots her a quick look over his shoulder. 'Long way from home to be falling in a canal,' he says.

The cabdriver stares but does not say a word when they pile in back with the dog.

'Um, I don't have any money,' says Mary.

'Don't worry about it,' says Randy. 'Let us take care of this.'

Mary catches PJ giving Randy a look but Randy's either ignoring him or too busy tending to the dog, who is panting now.

'She needs water,' he says.

Mary just nods. She's so overwhelmed by their kindness it's all she can do not to cry.

At the vet they have blankets, and Mary's wrapped in several, her wet clothes clinging to her underneath. The dog is in surgery. Just a puppy, no more than nine months old. She will lose an eye and some bones are broken but she's going to recover.

'She's a fighter,' the vet says, when he emerges to give them an update.

Randy has pulled out a flask of whiskey and he makes a show of offering it to Mary first.

'Um, no thanks,' she says, before she's even thought about it.

'You sure? C'mon, you're in shock - look how you're shaking.'

'No, really. I'm good.'

Mary's twisting the end of the blanket around her wrist. Wrapping it tight and watching her hand go purple, the blood vessels bulging. Thinks of when she was little and rode horses. The vet would come and clamp the horse's upper lip with steel pincers so it didn't feel the pain from the needle.

'Sure you're okay?' Randy says. 'Might want to get yourself looked at.' He's riffling through the brochures they have on display in reception. '10 reasons to neuter or spay your dog.'

'Yea, I'll be all right.' Mary releases the blanket and stares at her hand, all creased and red.

'Need to call anyone? Want to use my phone?'

'Ah, no.'

'You sure?'

'Yup.'

Randy shakes his head. Puts his phone away, looks down at the floor. Mary notices PJ has left the room. Stepped out for a cigarette. She can see him just through the window.

'Say, what do you think about this dog?' Randy asks, after a bit.

'Um, I don't know.'

Mary hasn't thought of it. Hasn't thought beyond being out of the canal. That's she's glad to be alive. That even for this brief while, she feels safe and looked after. Randy and PJ are so nice. It makes all the difference in the world.

'You should take her,' Mary says.

'You know, I was thinking...'

'Could you? I mean, or maybe you know someone...?'

'Yea, don't worry. The vet's not gonna go to all this trouble to save the dog's life just to have it put down.'

'Oh, true...'

'And I do have this niece. She's been begging my brother for a dog...'

Outside PJ has finished his smoke. Now he's pacing, on his cell phone.

'Talkin to his bird,' says Randy.

'Oh,' says Mary. 'Guess I kinda ruined your night.'

'Nah,' Randy shakes his head. He holds out his flask, so close Mary can smell the whiskey. 'You sure you don't want just a nip?'

She hesitates. 'No thanks, I'm good.'

***

'You can stop here.'

The cab drops her off in front of her flat. It's still dark, and halfway up the drive she trips. For that split second she is back in the canal - when she couldn't breathe, when she was deaf and weighted down.

Mary shudders. Her clothes are still damp and she smells. Wet jeans chafe the insides of her thighs.

Bangs on her front door. 'Jake?'

She doesn't expect him to answer - to be home. Darts outside again, goes around to the back of the building. The bathroom window is still open. She has to use a trash bin to reach it but she's able to crawl inside, scrapes her hips as she thunks down on the floor.

Calls out again, just in case, 'Jake?'

Her pants are off along with her underwear and now she's slipping out of her shirt, her bra. Finds the lights. The studio is empty - somehow she sensed it would be even as the cab was pulling up to the curb.

The bed unmade. Wine bottles stacked by the sink.

Naked, she returns to the bathroom. Bits of slime flattened to her body, her skin stained a faint orange - like she's soaked in turmeric. Covered in bruises.

Her face in the mirror is a shock. At the vet they'd cleaned up her gash, taped it in gauze, but now, as she takes it off, it's still seeping blood. Her forehead above her right eye is swollen, the skin a collage of red, purple, blue and yellow.

In the shower, for the first time in her life she can't take the water scalding hot. Even lukewarm, her scalp and cuts sting.

***

Without thinking, making a conscious decision, she begins to pack. Fits what she needs in her knapsack. What she can carry and still move fast. Finds her phone under the chair by the bed. Still no messages, no texts. Her laptop sits on the desk and she goes to it, opens it up. Clicks through to her email, defying the wave of fear and dread that sweeps through her. Her instincts are correct. A message from Jake, sent only hours before.

From: jakepverse@hotmail.com
To: Mary Cartwright <scarymary666@yahoo.com>
Subject: Dear Mary
Date: Tue, 29 May 2007 8:14 pm

Mary,

I know I fucked everything up and all I can do is say I'm so terribly sorry. I just freaked out about marriage, about JJ. I've wrecked people's lives, mine included. Please believe me, I am a complete mess. (Even the medication Paul gave me isn't working!)

Fuck. I hope one day you can forgive me, but I understand if you can't. I let myself get in too deep, but in the end, I have to do what I believe is the right thing.

Please try to remember all that was good...

Mary shuts the lid on her computer. It's dawn, and the sky is streaked with pink. Almost imperceptibly, the darkness has lifted.

Takes one last look around the flat. Jake's stuff is still strewn in the hall - his plays and poetry books, his notebooks, his socks. The striped scarf from her mother. His leopard print shirt - only Jake could pull it off. His wing-tipped shoes with the hole in the toe.

Now a few of her things are thrown into the mix. The biography of Jean Rhys. A box of charms. A Manchester A to Z.

Ira has her deposit and all the rent in advance. The last of her money. She pictures the cleaners, throwing out all that remains, readying the studio for the next tenant.

Mary hoists her knapsack on her back and steps into the hall, locking the door behind her. Slips the key under the mat and heads down the drive. Now the sky is colorless - in that void where it's neither dark enough nor light enough to cast a shadow.

Walking noiselessly in her Converse, she rounds the corner towards the bus station. The number 42 bus is there, engine running. Even though she's shivering with her wet hair, she knows it will be warm on board.

And she will take her seat at the back, by the window, where she can put her knees up and stare out at the houses and shops, the outskirts of the city just coming to life.

Nina-Marie Gardner's fiction has been published in 3AM Magazine and the anthologies Bedford Square and 3AM London, New York, Paris. She lives in Brooklyn.

Contact her at: nmgard@mac.com

Made in the USA
Charleston, SC
11 March 2011